Paul G. Wright

Print ISBNs
Amazon print 9780228633525
Ingram Spark 9780228633532
Barnes & Noble 9780228633549
BWL Print 9780228633556

BWL Publishing Inc.

Books we love to write ...
Authors around the world.
http://bwlpublishing.ca

Copyright 2024 by Paul G. Wright
Editor JD Shipton
Cover artist Pandora Designs

Acknowledgements

My thanks to:

Dana Hannah, Allison Jones, Ben Taylor, Patrick Cusick, Lavon Lacey, Diego Bruno, Lora Hanks, Dick Mays, Tim Norman, Eide Mays, Whit Harson, Bill Corley, Rhonda Farlowe, Howard Mears, Judson Vaughn, Marshall Peterson, Tara Wright, Steve Wright, Virginia Wright, Todd Ford, Dan Lawton, Brian Petrucelli, Mike Tuffley

James West, Ph.D., Electrical Engineering

Captain (Ret.) JD Shipton, Royal Canadian Air Force (RCAF)

Sergeant Charles E. Gray, United States Marine Corps (1993–1999)

Staff Sergeant Shaun Mills, US Army (1989–2014)

Sergeant Bruce Swain, Snellville Police Force

SPYCRAFT: Essentials Bayard & Holmes (June 18, 2018)

Table of Contents

Chapter 1

The file lay in easy reach, on the conference table. The letters LMAR printed across the front. In another moment she would have it. She reached out.

"I think not."

Mason. He was like a cat, with more lives.

"You think wrong," said Vogel.

Mason's hand slammed down on the folder, inches from hers. Their eyes met—his with that same arrogant smirk she'd seen a hundred times before, his dark hair perfectly in place. As always, he was impeccably dressed, his wine-red tie in a flawless knot. Vogel couldn't deny it—under different circumstances, she might . . . But no, he was an international criminal and a murderer. And he kissed like a college freshman. The lines were drawn.

Mason looked at her through steely eyes. "Vogel," he said coolly, "why do we always seem to have this same discussion?"

Vogel smirked. "Because, Mason, you're terrible at losing."

Mason nodded. "A character flaw, I'm afraid, that is permanent."

She snatched the file away as Mason lunged for her. Instinctively, her hand went for her gun, and she pointed the sleek black barrel directly at his head. He froze, a smile playing across his face.

"Now let's be practical," Mason said. "There's no way out."

"You always say that."

A door opened and men in dark fatigues entered, holding assault rifles. Mason's henchmen. She should have known. They stood on either side of him, with their weapons trained on her like spiders. Vogel counted six in all.

Mason eyed her. "Really, Vogel. I mean, what are your options? Why don't you just hand that over and we can all sit down?"

A bead of sweat ran down her back. Her shoes were tight, and she hadn't showered since Wednesday. She felt gross. This was taking longer than expected. They were on the thirtieth floor, standing in front of a series of plate glass windows. Mason was right. There was no way out.

It was then she heard the roar of the helicopter.

* * *

The pilot held the machine in a hover, across from the building. A black metal bird against the night sky. "Approaching extraction zone—300 meters out," his voice clipped through the comms. "Holding steady."

The mission was not taking place. Nothing that was happening now would be part of any official record.

"Visual confirmed." The door gunner crouched in position, his eye on the thermal optic. Everything glowed green. The transponder on Agent Vogel's belt had given them her position. Vogel was to his left, with a group of armed men behind her. Mason on the right. The shooter placed the crosshairs between them. The objective was not to kill. Rather, to rescue.

* * *

"Hostiles spotted. Waiting on your go." Vogel heard the voice in her earpiece and ducked.

Mason saw the flash and barely had enough time to leap out of the way before the explosion shattered the window. A hail of glass rained down, and a small canister dropped onto the floor. Steel spikes sprang from its sides, holding it in place, as smoke poured from one end.

Vogel held her breath and grabbed the can with the Kevlar-reinforced cable, attached to it. Her eyes stung as she secured the D-ring to her belt. Even breathing through her nose felt like inhaling fire.

Getting to her feet she snatched the folder from the rubble. The hard part was still to come. Turning to the shattered window Vogel faced a gaping hole that opened to the night sky. The helicopter hovered just thirty yards away, its side door wide open, beckoning.

"It's been lovely," she said, turning to Mason, "but I have a flight to catch."

Mason coughed through the smoke as Vogel pressed the button on her transponder. The chopper began to rise.

Stepping to the edge, she took a deep breath and wished she'd chosen a normal profession, like Kristy Hubbard. Closing her eyes, she swallowed hard— and leaped. Vogel hated heights.

Cold air whipped around her, and she had the desperate feeling of plummeting to her death. Then suddenly, the cable snapped taught and she was flying beneath the huge machine. The rhythm of the rotor beating like a drum. Her heart raced as she grabbed the Kevlar, clinging to it she breathed the thick smell of Jet-A exhaust and looked down at the city.

Wind tore through her hair and a rush of adrenaline shot through her body. No, she thought, as she was slowly winched upward, she made the right choice. Let Kristy Hubbard try this.

Mason's eyes burned as he peered through the haze, watching. It was a disaster, of course . . . and yet he had to admire her style. He admired everything about Agent Vogel. The helicopter moved away, and he rubbed his eyes as a breeze blew the remains of smoke from the room.

"Clever, Vogel," he said, quietly. "Extremely clever."

* * *

Strong hands gripped her arms, yanking her into the chopper. The roar of the rotors filled her ears as she unclipped the harness. The door slammed shut as Vogel got to her feet, breathless.

"Are you all right?"

Looking up, she recognized Archer, the director of operations. Her back stiffened. "Mission complete, sir," she replied, handing him the folder.

The cabin swayed as Archer skimmed the file, eyes narrowing in thought. "We're heading back to Washington. I want Twelve to see this firsthand."

"Understood, sir," she nodded.

The director shut the folder and offered a rare smile. "Take a seat, Vogel. You need anything?"

Vogel gave him a weary look. "A drink would be nice, sir."

* * *

The agency headquarters looked more like a nondescript office building than a den of operatives and espionage planners. A generic modern glass and brick building, in lower Washington D.C., it blended in seamlessly with the surrounding skyscrapers and could pass for the headquarters of any major company - which was largely the point.

Vogel had arrived early and had already gulped down a Danish and two cups of coffee. This succeeded in twisting her stomach into a knot. She stood in front of the restroom mirror and stared at her reflection. She was thirty years old with sandy, shoulder-length blond hair and blue eyes. Eyes, she had been told, that could be warm or deadly cold. There was tension in her face, no doubt about it, and her makeup had been a rush job. But then again, that same person had said she didn't need makeup.

She took a step back and evaluated things one last time. A gray business suit with black flats and a cream-colored blouse.

That always seemed to work. She wasn't happy with her hair, as she hadn't been to a stylist in months. It would have to wait. The head of the department wanted a briefing, and this always meant one of two things: either the assignment had been a success, or it hadn't. She never knew until she sat down and Twelve looked at her. If the mission wasn't a success, there would be hard questions. That part still made her nervous.

"All right," she said to her reflection. "Show time." Vogel dug into her purse and produced two pink pills for stomach distress. She swallowed them with water from a paper cup and washed her hands. As she dried them, the door opened, and another woman walked in. She recognized her as Delta.

"Hi Lora," Delta smiled, joining her at the sink.

"Hi, Kim."

Delta sat her purse on the counter and noticed Vogel's portfolio beside it. "Big day?"

"Very."

Delta nodded and turned to the mirror. "Don't worry, you'll do fine."

Vogel sighed. She hoped so.

* * *

The office of the department head looked exactly as one would expect. Oak desk and thick carpeting, a leather couch no one sat on, and an abstract painting by some obscure artist. Lamps sat on marble end tables with an impressive bookcase with interior lighting as the backdrop. Knickknacks were arranged on the shelves between thick, leather volumes. Vogel glanced at them as she sat on the other side of the desk and wondered if anyone had ever read them. Were they even real?

Vogel crossed her legs for the third time, watching as Twelve scrutinized her report through those librarian glasses. The silence stretched, thick and uncomfortable. Once, Twelve had glanced up to make a note, but otherwise, she hadn't said a word. Vogel never knew how to handle these moments— it felt like meeting the parents on a first date, awkward and dangerous. Her feet were freezing in her flats, and hunger gnawed at her stomach, which let out a low growl. She coughed, hoping Twelve hadn't noticed.

If she did, Twelve didn't acknowledge it. Instead, she looked up from the report. Twelve was older, with short white hair and a stare that could freeze water. Vogel felt the same way now as she'd felt in the principal's office when she was a kid. Scared to death.

"This is very good work, Vogel," Twelve said after a moment. "Very impressive."

"Thank you."

"I'm not sure we needed the Hollywood ending, but then again, Mason does have a tendency for the melodramatic."

"He has a tendency to be a horse's ass," Vogel blurted before she could catch herself. She bit her lip and Twelve was expressionless as if deciding whether to react.

"Quite," Twelve said, finally, and closed the folder. "Lora?"

"Yes?" It was slightly unusual for Twelve not to address her by her code name.

"How have you been?"

"Been?"

"Yes, how are things going?"

Vogel stared at her blankly. "I don't understand."

"How are you feeling lately?"

"All right, I suppose. Maybe a little fatigued."

"Trouble sleeping?"

That was an understatement. She was lucky if she got four hours' worth a night. "Well, actually, now that you mention it, yes."

"I don't doubt it." Twelve reached for another folder. This one was red. "According to this, in the last three months, you've been to England, Thailand, and South America. You've completed thirteen assignments and volunteered for additional work in Austria."

Had she really been on thirteen missions?

"Your last vacation was more than a year ago"—Twelve was still reading—"and you haven't taken a personal trip in five months."

Vogel's stomach chirped again, but this time Twelve was busy shuffling papers.

"Vogel," Twelve said, adjusting her glasses. "Your dedication to the agency is admirable. You're one of our best operatives and your service record is exemplary."

"Have I done something wrong?"

"No. We'd be having a very different conversation if that were the case. But there's more to life than work and dedication to the agency." She closed the folder and looked at Vogel. "When was the last time you saw Richard Davis?"

The question took her by surprise. "Richard?"

Twelve nodded. "Richard Davis. American. Thirty-two. Nice-looking, with dark hair. Writes for a small Florida newspaper."

"The Chronicle," Vogel mumbled.

"Exactly. And he's also single, according to our most current information."

Vogel's chair was suddenly uncomfortable. She squirmed in it. "Twelve, I—"

"When?" The look on Twelve's face was firm.

"We . . . got together in February. For Valentine's Day, as a matter of fact."

"And?"

Vogel met Twelve's eyes, then dropped them to her lap. "It didn't go well."

"I see."

Vogel swallowed. "With all due respect, I really don't see what any of this has to do with—"

Twelve was already reaching for another folder. "Lora,"—she used the name again—"this agency functions as a team."

Oh, please not the speech again. Not now. All she wanted to do was just sit at her desk and catch up on paperwork. Maybe eat something chocolate.

"And each member of that team is expected to be at their best mentally, physically, and emotionally. Do you understand?"

"Yes . . . ma'am."

"Good. Because part of my job is making sure my agents are paying attention to these things."

"Well, I always try to eat a balanced diet."

"I'm sure you do. But that's not exactly what I mean." She opened a blue folder. "I'm giving you a new assignment."

Vogel instantly felt better. "Oh, thank you! Where am I going?"

"Lancaster, Florida."

Her stomach twisted sideways. "Where?"

"You heard me. There's a chemistry professor at the university who claims he has cracked the invisibility problem. Your job is to investigate and report your findings. If there are any."

It was a setup. Vogel didn't like setups. Lancaster was where Richard lived. "But that's field research. First-year stuff. Any of the new recruits could—"

"He's a leader in his field and you already know the area. This may just turn out to be something, Vogel. If it does, I want someone who's an expert. Someone I can count on."

"Yes, ma'am." There was a sinking feeling in her chest that went all the way to her shoes.

"Your contact is Simon Blackmarr. He's giving a lecture at the university tonight on his findings. You are to make contact with him and report on these findings." Twelve handed the folder to Vogel, who nodded limply.

"Understood."

Twelve removed her glasses and managed a weak smile. "Sit on the beach, Lora. Lay in the sun. Drink one of those concoctions with the paper umbrellas and look at the ocean. Take some downtime. There will be plenty of work waiting when you come back. You have my word that I won't give Mason to anyone else."

Vogel frowned inwardly and put the folder under her arm. "Is that all?"

"That's all," said Twelve, turning back to her work. "Dismissed."

It was like being a teenager who'd just been sentenced to detention. Vogel slipped her purse over her shoulder and stalked out of the office. She would fly to Lancaster, she would talk with the stupid professor, evaluate his work, and complete the assignment. But she wouldn't contact Richard Davis, and she would not have a nice time.

Chapter 2

Richard Davis had been at The Lancaster Chronicle, off and on, for five years. He kept saying he was going to get out of it.

And he meant it.

There were other papers, and he'd had other offers. The problem was, it would mean giving up his rent-controlled, two-bedroom apartment, with a view of the Gulf of Mexico. And that was a hard give up. Davis loved the beach. Loved taking a dip after a lousy day at work, and loved sitting on the shore in the evening, with a beer, watching the sun drop into the sea.

He had a dead-end job, a cheap car, and so-so living quarters, but he had the beach. And that was more than most people had. So, he dealt with it.

Davis took a bite of the ham sandwich from Andie's and turned back to the computer monitor on his desk. He was writing another story about a city council meeting.

He knew why.

It was payback for that incident with the parking commissioner two months ago. It wasn't his fault. He'd just reported the facts. How could he have known the man was going to have his editor's car towed?

Davis chewed the sandwich and tried to think of something interesting to say about the coming improvements to the city's sewer system. There really wasn't anything. He was still chewing when the phone rang.

"This is Davis," he said into the receiver.

"What?!" a female voice yelled, on the other end of the phone.

Davis looked into the earpiece. "Come again?"

"I didn't tell anybody I was going to be here. This is strictly business. Now, what do you want?"

He sat up. "Vogel?"

"Who else?!" she said. "And how the hell did you know I was here?"

"I didn't. I don't. Where are you?"

"Here!" said Vogel. "At the Masters Hotel on Fourth Street. The company suite. I check in, get my room key, and the first thing they tell me is someone at The Lancaster Chronicle would like me to call mister Richard Davis. Now, what's this all about?"

She got loud when she was upset. Davis held the phone away from his ear.

"Vogel, calm down."

"I am calm!"

"Look, I didn't call anybody, I swear. Whoever it was, it wasn't me."

"I'll bet."

Davis winced. "So, how are you?"

"Lousy!" Vogel's line went dead.

He rubbed his temples with his forefingers and replaced the receiver.

Vogel.

No. They weren't doing that again.

No, thank you.

He had a nice, simple thing going with the waitress at Andie's. She was cute, average, and gave him an extra cookie with his ham sandwich. She also thought writing for the paper was exciting, even if it was about sewer systems.

Forget it.

It wasn't happening.

He took a sip of cold coffee and refocused on the story. He typed: Things will soon be moving faster than ever in Lancaster . . . The phone rang again.

"Davis," he said, wedging the receiver between his ear and shoulder.

There was a pause.

"That pizza place over on Harris doesn't deliver anymore," said Vogel.

"I know. They stopped a couple of months ago. The owner's kid started college."

"I really wanted a large supreme."

"A supreme would be good."

Another pause.

"I guess I could probably go get it myself."

"You probably could."

"I'll get the staff to do it"

"That's another idea."

Silence.

"I don't like you anymore," said Vogel.

The line went dead again.

Davis replaced the receiver and went back to the story. A shower of improvements will soon be descending on . . .

The desk phone rang again. David sighed.

"Davis," he re-wedged the receiver.

"The staff won't do it," said Vogel. "Something about policy."

"That stinks."

"It's stupid. You have room service, why can't you send one of these dopes over there to get a lousy pizza? The company would pay for it."

"You want me to write an article about it?"

"Shut up. I'm not talking to you."

"Sorry, I got confused." Davis continued typing on the keyboard. He could hear her walking around her room, unpacking. "What are you in town for?"

"Nothing. Nothing important, anyway. They think I'm working too hard."

"Are you?"

"No. Do you want to have dinner?"

Davis moved the receiver to his other ear. "Can't."

"Why not?"

"I've got a date." He grinned. "I'm taking her to a movie."

Vogel hung up.

Back to his computer. A river of new developments will soon be flooding Lancaster . . .

The phone exploded.

"With who?!" Vogel said before he could even answer.

"What?"

"Who are you going out with?"

Davis leaned back in his chair. "Her name is Cathy."

"Cathy?!"

"Cathy Rogers."

"What does she do?"

"Works at Andie's. She rings up my sandwiches. Gives me a free cookie."

Vogel said something Davis couldn't print on the front page.

"Anyhow, it was good to hear from you. Keep in touch."

"Davis, you get over here and pick me up in ten minutes!"

* * *

Alfonzo's was located on Lakewood Drive. It was Italian and upscale, which is what Vogel wanted. Davis had even put on his coat and straightened his tie. The waiter led them to a spot by the window, with a white tablecloth. Vogel sat down and hung her purse on the back of her chair. Davis picked up a menu and pretended to study it. Vogel glared at him, still irritated.

24

"Cathy Rogers?!" she finally said.

Davis put down the menu. "You said in the car you didn't want to talk about it."

"I don't. I'm not. Forget it. What do you eat here?"

"Italian food."

"I don't want Italian," she said, grabbing her purse. "Let's go somewhere else."

"Vogel, come on." Davis reached over the table and put his hand on her arm. She looked at him.

"All right." She replaced the purse. "Just don't call me Lora anymore. I don't like it."

"I didn't."

"I thought you did."

She stared at the menu and had no idea what any of it said. The waiter appeared. He was a thin man with little hair and was dressed in a wine-red suit. Vogel didn't like him.

"Good evening, my name is Oliver. I'll be your server tonight. Can I start you off with something?"

"I'll have a scotch and soda," said Davis.

"Very good," breathed Oliver. "And for you miss?"

"Double bourbon. Neat."

She looked at the waiter as if he were Mason on the other end of her gun and he shivered.

"Yes ma'am," Oliver said and quickly scurried away.

"Will you calm down?" Davis said, laying his menu on the table. "This was your idea, remember?"

"No, it wasn't. It was her idea," said Vogel. "The whole thing was her idea."

"Who?"

"Never mind." She wanted a cigarette. She had been trying to quit for over a year but at times like this, she really wanted a cigarette. Unfortunately, she didn't have any. "A sandwich shop chick?" she finally said. "Really?"

"What do you care? You didn't want to get serious, remember? It was too much of an inconvenience."

"I have a job, Richard."

"So do I."

"It takes me all over the place. I never know where I'm going to be going, or what I'm going to be doing."

"Neither do I. My editor has me running down story leads every day. I never know where I'm going to wind up."

"It's not the same thing."

"It's exactly the same thing. The difference is, Cathy is okay with it."

"Cathy doesn't have to worry about leaping out of a window, with a gun pointed at her head."

Oliver returned and nervously set the drinks in front of them.

"Thank you," said Davis.

"Are we ready to order?" asked the waiter.

Vogel still had no idea.

"Could you give us a few more minutes?" asked Davis.

"With pleasure, sir." The man practically sprinted from the table. Davis had the feeling he was going to call the police.

"Will you relax?" he hissed. "You're not at the F.B.I. now."

"I don't work for the F.B.I. See? You can't even remember that. No wonder I dumped you."

"You didn't dump me, I ran away. Screaming."

"Like hell. Where did the flowers come from? And the card. 'My darling, Lora. I count the days, the hours, the minutes—'"

"All right—"

"After I'd told you a million times, I hate being called Lora!"

"Alright, already!" People at another table looked in their direction and Davis covered the side of his face with his hand. "Look, let's just forget it, okay? What do you want to eat?"

Vogel shrugged, indifferent. "I don't care. Just order something for me."

Oliver tiptoed cautiously back to the table. A deliberately non-threatening smile plastered across his face. "So," he said, in the tone people use to calm wild animals. "Are we ready to order yet?"

Davis nodded. "I believe so. We'll have two Caesar salads, two servings of the cannelloni, and a bottle of Merlot."

Oliver jotted everything down and nodded, approvingly. "Very good, sir," he said, taking their menus. "I'll be back with your salads."

Vogel smiled to herself. Davis had remembered her favorite dish.

* * *

They had met several years ago by accident. Davis had been writing a series of stories on key city leaders. During the process, he had taken a photo that, for reasons he still didn't fully understand, was explosive. Vogel had been sent to prevent its appearance in the newspaper. How the agency had known of its existence was never explained. By pure luck, their paths crossed. It was after hours, and he had forgotten something at the office. Turning on the light, he caught her with the negative. In a rare moment of candor, she confessed, but it was only after seeing her credentials as an operative that Davis was convinced not to call the authorities.

Instead, out of mutual respect, they agreed to a cup of coffee. She wasn't what he'd expected. A bit guarded at first, but she warmed up quickly and seemed genuinely glad to have someone to talk to. On a hunch, Davis had written his phone number on a scrap of paper and slid it across the table. Vogel looked at it for several seconds, surprised, and finally tucked it into her purse. She smiled at him, sideways, and asked the waitress for another cup of coffee. That was when he first knew.

It had been a warm afternoon in May when she told him her real name was Lora and that she had gone to high school in Connecticut. Their first date was pizza and a movie and their first

kiss had been under a tree in the park. She blushed, tried to hide behind her hair, and finally kissed him back.

Two and a half years, later they were having dinner at Alfonzo's, and he still didn't know what to make of her. Part of it, of course, was her job. That would always remain a mystery. Where exactly did she work, for example? The agency was called Psi, after the twenty-third letter of the Greek alphabet. She'd shown him her badge and identity card one evening on the sofa, along with her gun.

Officially they didn't exist. At least, not in the phone book, and not under any government listing he'd ever seen. He knew the organization fell under the auspices of the intelligence community, but precisely how and where was unclear. The most she would say was that they handled "gray work." From what he could tell, this included such things as manipulating governments, dictators, evil organizations, corrupt industrialists, and crime lords. Along with various other projects.

He listened to her stories, the ones she could tell, and marveled at all of it. It was hard to believe the woman who was ticklish behind her ribcage and liked cartoons and AC/DC could leap from a burning building or parachute into a foreign country to steal secret documents.

The other part was less easy to pin down. The agent was the most visible part of her, but it was only one part. There was a whole other section she kept hidden behind the cloak and dagger. It was that person he was fascinated by and attracted to. The same person she'd let him see at the diner that first night. The one who couldn't remember the punch line to jokes and told stories of smoking in the girls' restroom in eighth grade.

It was that person he wanted to know more about, and that was the one she felt the least comfortable showing.

Which was why they hadn't spoken since February.

Dinner arrived and Vogel waited until she started her cannelloni before she asked him. "Are you busy tonight?"

He had a forkful of salad but set it down. With Vogel, this was always a loaded question. "Why?"

She shrugged. "There's this thing I've got to go to for work. I thought maybe . . . we could go together. If you want."

"What kind of thing?"

"A lecture thing."

"A lecture thing?" Davis felt like a parrot. "What's that?"

Vogel wiped the corner of her mouth with her napkin and rolled her eyes. "It's nonsense. Some professor at the university says he's found the key to the invisibility problem. He's giving a lecture on it tonight and they want me to check it out."

"Invisibility," he said slowly. "You mean as in, the invisible man stuff?"

"It's just an excuse for Twelve to make me take some time off. We get these kinds of reports all the time. They never go anywhere, but we still have to check them out. I just thought you might want to come along."

Somebody was playing the piano in another part of the restaurant. The tune was familiar

but he couldn't name it. He actually had nothing planned for the evening. Just a walk on the beach. "Invisibility," he said again. "That's not something you hear about every day."

"I'll buy you a drink if you say yes."

"How about a cup of coffee instead? At Morty's."

Morty's was the diner they'd first frequented. Vogel put her glass down and looked at the tablecloth. A smile played at her lips and Davis thought he saw a tinge of red in her cheeks, but it could have been the wine.

"All right," she finally said, looking at him. "But no cream."

* * *

Vogel sat in the passenger seat of Davis' used car as it turned onto the campus of Lancaster State University. It was a medium-sized school with a decent reputation. Davis had gone there for a semester or two, as an undergraduate, before transferring out of state. Vogel held her purse in her lap as he turned the car into a space behind the Oxnard Building. She still thought his car smelled like burnt vinyl.

They got out and began walking across the parking lot. Vogel wore a black blouse, with a pair of gray slacks and matching blazer. Her boots made a crunching sound on the pavement.

"So, what do you do these days?" he asked her.

"What do you mean?"

"I mean, how are things going?"

Vogel shrugged. "Okay, I guess. I go to work, I do my job, and I get paid. It's a living."

"Are you happy with it?"

"With what?"

"Life."

"I could ask you the same thing."

"You did. And I told you, I'm content with the status quo."

"Content is not the same thing as happy."

"No, it's not. It's an acceptance of one's state. I have a job I don't hate, and I have an apartment that's rent-controlled, with a view most people only get to see once or twice a year, in a part of the country you're only supposed to live in when you retire. This isn't a bad fate to be content with."

"But you're still not happy."

"Neither are you."

"Give me a cigarette."

"I stopped smoking," Davis said, as he stepped onto the sidewalk.

"You're a twerp."

It was odd the way things fell back together. She even let him slip his arm around her waist. It was comfortable and the truth was, she liked it. Despite all the frustration and handwringing about the job and commitment, she liked Davis. Liked being with him and feeling normal. When she was with Davis, she could go to dinner. Watch TV. Talk on the phone or walk on the beach.

All with a friend.

And . . . yes, that was how she wanted to think of him. Which was the whole problem because she did sort of want a relationship. Even with the headaches, hassles, and aggravation that went with it. Particularly now. It had become important and was like a fly or mosquito that she couldn't quite shake.

The problem was her. At least, it seemed to be. Some people in the world were solitaires and she'd come to accept that maybe she was part of that crowd. She had flunked Romance 101 in high school or missed taking it altogether because she simply didn't know how to do it. Things just never seemed to click, even when she wore lipstick.

And that frustrated her.

Davis was attractive and she knew he thought the same of her. That was another problem. She really enjoyed being with him and the movies, pizza, and laughing together were all great. But when they would talk in the car or be alone on the sofa, she felt . . . awkward. It was something she'd never discussed with him because she couldn't think of a way to do it that wouldn't sound weird or make him feel like it wasn't his fault. The truth was, she wasn't very good at hugging and kissing. Wasn't comfortable letting people get that close. Instead, she just tried to avoid it as much as possible.

The other issue was her job. She dropped in and out of his life like a yo-yo. He said he was fine with it, but what man would want a woman who was always running off to save the world? In a way, she could understand his interest in the sandwich shop girl. This Cathy person sounded normal and could be there for him. Vogel didn't have anything to offer but aggravation. At least that was the way she saw it.

They approached the entrance and Davis took his hand from her side and opened the door. Vogel stepped through it.

No, she thought to herself, they were not getting back together.

Chapter 3

Professor Simon Blackmarr was a modest man who did not enjoy giving lectures. He never quite knew what to say and needed everything written down. His notes frequently got jumbled and he tended to lose his place, often leaving him searching through papers in the middle of an important point.

Giving speeches was not his strong suit and he preferred the classroom, where he could dialogue with his students. Or better still, the laboratory, where he could focus his attention on solving a single problem. No distractions, no interruptions, just the work. Time would simply melt away.

Unfortunately, the university required these talks. Once a semester, he was expected to give a detailed account of his research and report his findings. It was as dull for him as it was for the poor souls who attended. Turnout was usually sparse—just faculty and those students currently taking his classes. Occasionally, some of his peers dropped in, and now and then a few curious civilians, but not much more.

Tonight, promised to be no different.

He'd made an interesting discovery that could have some unique applications, but it was still in the earliest stages. Further research and further testing were required before a final analysis could be reached. Which was why he disliked mentioning it.

But it was required.

Simon sighed as he looked over the handwritten pages and adjusted his spectacles. He could be home watching TV now or taking a walk. He stood in the wings as Dr. Stewart introduced him. Dr. Stewart spoke in a stiff monotone and was shaped like a pear. Blackmarr didn't care for her. She waddled when she moved and was never satisfied with any answer you gave her.

"And now without further ado," wheezed Stewart. "Professor Simon Blackmarr."

He looked upward and winced. On with the show.

* * *

The two men seated near the back of the hall were not students. Neither were they members of the professor's peer group. They were also not residents of Lancaster. But they were curious and politely applauded as the professor stepped onto the stage and walked to the podium. The dark-haired one had a sharp nose and an angular chin. The white-haired one had hazel eyes, which he trained on the small man onstage. He watched as the man fumbled with his papers and adjusted the microphone.

"Good evening," he finally managed. "The current attitude in physics seems to be to absolutely avoid anything dealing with 'Field Effects.'"

* * *

Davis sat in the theater chair next to Vogel and tried to seem interested in the professor mumbling at the lectern. He had no idea what was being said and the fellow talking was one of the most boring people he'd ever listened to.

" . . . dealing with 'E-field'; 'H-field'; and 'M-field' effects," the man droned on, "this is of interest because no one has significantly explained the basics of . . ."

Davis tapped Vogel on the arm.

"How much of this do you have to sit through?" he asked in a low voice.

"All of it," she whispered.

"How will they know if you don't?"

"Shhh." She waved him quiet.

Blackmarr was speaking again. " . . . utilizing an 'M field,' which captures the surrounding molecules." He muttered something else incomprehensible and began reading from a new piece of paper. " . . . indicating that this 'M field' functions on two different air densities. The molecules become compact due to humidity and magnetic attraction creating a molecular mirror."

If Vogel hadn't sworn softly, Davis would never have known anything significant had happened. He glanced over and saw that she was pressed back into the chair with her eyes wide open.

Vogel's breath caught in her throat. "He's done it," she whispered.

"Done what?"

Blackmarr was still reading, and she turned to him with a disturbed look. "Davis, this may be a little more complicated than I thought."

Davis frowned. "Vogel, what's going on?"

"Let's get out of here. I'll explain it in the hall."

They slipped quietly out of the aisle and headed for one of the side doors.

No one noticed that the chairs the two strangers had been sitting in were now empty.

* * *

"You mean to tell me that you actually understood what that guy was saying?" Davis was trying to keep up with Vogel, as they hurried down one of the hallways leading to the rear of the stage.

"Parts of it, yes. And that's what worries me."

"So, what did he say?"

Vogel stopped and looked around cautiously. She stepped closer to Davis and leaned in. "That he's solved it. He's actually cracked the invisibility problem."

Davis raised an eyebrow. "You mean, for real? No magic tricks or anything?"

She nodded soberly. "I think so."

"Holy cow." He swallowed.

"Exactly. Now you see the problem."

Davis did see the problem. It was the equivalent of the discovery of fire. Vogel started walking again and he followed. "So, what are you going to do?"

"I don't know. The first thing I've got to do is check it out."

* * *

Simon was exhausted. The lecture had been a disaster, leaving him drained and frustrated. All he wanted to do now was go home, pour a tall drink, and watch something on television. Preferably something animated.

He stepped out of the wing, picked up his briefcase, and stuffed the disorganized notes into one of the side pockets. Sweat ran down his back and he felt a shooting pain between his eyes. He closed them and rubbed the bridge of his nose. When he opened them again, two people stood in front of him. A man and a woman. The man was slightly taller, with dark hair. The woman had sand-colored hair and blue eyes, she looked at him intently.

"Yes?" he said, a little puzzled.

"Professor, I wanted to congratulate you on your lecture and your discovery," she said, in one breath. "It's a remarkable achievement."

"Thank you, thank you." Simon waved, trying to get away.

"I wonder if I could have a moment to ask you a few questions about it?"

"I'm sorry, my dear, but I'm very tired and it's been a long day," he said, trying to move past. "If you'll excuse me."

The woman blocked him. "This will only take a few minutes." Her hand moved to her purse, and she produced credentials he'd never seen before.

Nevertheless, they were the kind one couldn't ignore.

"Yes," he said with a nod. "Yes, of course."

* * *

Vogel followed Davis and the professor into a nearby classroom. He switched on a light and put his briefcase on the desk. Vogel closed the door and locked it.

"You're from the government?" Blackmarr asked, looking nervous.

"In a manner of speaking," said Vogel.

"What do you want?"

"My name is Vogel. I've been sent to ascertain whether your discovery is legitimate and to report your findings."

"Why?"

"For security reasons."

Blackmarr seemed confused. "Security?"

"I'll explain in a moment," she said. "About your discovery."

The professor shrugged. "I'd hardly call it a discovery. As I mentioned in the lecture, it was more of an accident. The formula reacted in an unexpected way and demonstrated new properties. It's still in the early stages of testing, however."

"This formula," said Davis. "Does it really make things invisible?"

Blackmarr stared at him blankly. "Well . . . yes, I suppose so. When the surface temperature rises above thirty-two degrees Fahrenheit, the material becomes translucent. The suspended micro particles generate an 'M field', and anything coming in contact is affected by the field."

Davis looked at Vogel and then back at the professor. "What does that mean, exactly?"

Blackmarr sighed. "Here, let me show you."

He opened a pouch on the side of his briefcase and removed a small plastic container. "I used this in my afternoon class," he said, setting the container on the desk. Blackmarr assumed the air of an instructor. "The specimen is being kept at a temperature under thirty-two degrees Fahrenheit. You'll notice that when I remove it, it's visible and has a slight blue cast."

Vogel and Davis watched with interest as Simon opened the container and extracted something resembling a cube. He placed a glass slide that had been coated with a dark material on the desktop and set the cube on top of it. Vogel noticed that it did seem to have a light, unearthly blue color.

"Now, observe closely," Blackmarr said, a note of pride creeping into his voice. "As the surface temperature rises above thirty-two degrees, the material undergoes a transformation."

The three looked on, and as they did the cube began to shimmer, its edges softening. Then, as if swallowed by the air itself, it disappeared entirely, leaving only an unsettling void. Vogel gasped and put a hand in the direction of the spot.

"I can still feel it," she said.

"Of course," said the professor. "Nothing has changed about the specimen except its appearance. Its mass is still intact in every detail."

Davis tapped the spot with his finger and looked at Blackmarr. "You said something about an 'M field'?"

"Ahh, yes!" he said, raising a finger. "This is one of the most interesting developments. When the material's temperature rises above thirty-two degrees, the suspended micro particles generate a high-density polarized 'M field,' capturing the surrounding molecules and magnetically making them compact. Notice here." Blackmarr took a pen from his coat pocket and set it atop the unseen cube. It immediately vanished.

Vogel squeaked.

Davis reached for the pen and as he moved it from the cube, it appeared to rematerialize in his hand. "Incredible."

Blackmarr beamed. "Not really. Just a matter of simple physics. As I mentioned before, the field utilizes two different air densities, creating a type of mirror."

"But what about that piece of glass underneath?" said Davis, looking closely. "Why can I still see that?"

The professor nodded animatedly. "Very good, very good. That's an excellent point. I was surprised by this myself. You see, the slide is coated with blue eupharedite, which as we know inhibits certain—"

"How much of this material exists?" Vogel said, cautiously.

The professor frowned at her over his glasses, apparently irritated at being interrupted. "Just the original sample," he said. "I haven't finished testing it."

"And this is a type of metal?" Vogel asked, feeling for the edges of the cube.

"In a sense. A magnetic molecular compound would be a more accurate description. Go ahead and pick it up. I want to demonstrate something to your friend."

Vogel lifted the cube.

As she did, a strange mist descended on the world, and everything in it lost its color. She could see a faint outline of the cube in her hand, but reality had suddenly turned black and white.

"Vogel!" Davis shouted. He dropped the pen and looked scared. "Vogel, are you okay?"

"Yes?" she said. "What's going on?"

"There! You see?" the professor said triumphantly. "When the 'M field' is amplified by the body's own electrical system, the effect is complete."

"Professor, this is really strange. It's like the color has run out of everything," said Vogel.

"You can put the cube down now," said Blackmarr. "Everything is fine."

She set it back on the glass slide and the world returned to normal. Davis gasped and his eyes nearly jumped from his head.

"Oh, there you are," he said, with a worried look.

"What's the matter with you?" said Vogel. "You look like you've seen a ghost."

"That's an understatement," said Davis.

"What do you mean?"

"Vogel, you just disappeared."

She blinked. "I did what?"

"I was staring right at you when you picked up the cube. You disappeared, just like that pen."

She looked around, then shook her head. "You're kidding."

"No, he's not," Blackmarr said, reaching for the cube. "Observe."

A second later, there was no professor. Simply a disembodied voice coming from the place where the professor had stood. Vogel was astonished.

"As I mentioned before," the professor's voice continued, "the 'M field' is amplified by the body's electrical system. Which means that as long as the material is in contact with the body itself, the effect is complete. When I set the cube back down, of course,"— Blackmarr reappeared—"the field is broken."

"Goodnight!" Vogel said, dropping her purse.

Blackmarr grinned, happily at first, and then paused. They were both gaping at him as if he had some strange disfigurement. "What's the matter?" he asked.

"Professor," Vogel began, slowly. "I think perhaps you need to come with us."

He gave her a perplexed look. "Come with you? Where?"

"To Washington."

"What on earth for?"

"Among other things, to keep you alive."

Chapter 4

"I don't understand any of this," Blackmarr muttered, as he led Davis and Vogel down the hall to his laboratory. "This is a minor discovery, in a minor university, by a minor researcher. Why should anybody be interested in it?"

"Professor, you don't understand the implications of what you've uncovered," said Vogel. "Mankind has been searching for invisibility since the beginning of civilization. It's the ultimate camouflage. Armies could approach nations undetected. Ships and planes could attack without fear. Snipers could eliminate their targets from inches away. The possibilities are as limitless as they are terrifying and there isn't a government anywhere that wouldn't kill you for this knowledge."

"But it hasn't been tested," Simon protested. "It's in the most experimental stages."

"That doesn't matter," said Davis. "It exists and people know about it."

They reached the door to the lab and found it forced open. Splinters from the frame scattered across the tile floor, as though someone had kicked it in.

"What is this?!" Blackmarr said in surprise. He started inside but Vogel stopped him.

"Wait," Vogel whispered, her instincts flaring. Something was off—very off. Her hand slipped the gun from her shoulder holster.

Davis stared at her. "What are you doing?"

"I'm on duty now," said Vogel, disengaging the safety. "Both of you get behind me."

Davis and the professor followed at a safe distance, as she crossed the threshold. Switching on the overhead lights, Vogel swept the room with the automatic.

The place was trashed. Shattered bottles and overturned testing equipment littered the floor. A filing cabinet had been flung open and wind from a shattered window sent papers whirling toward the ceiling. A chill ran down her spine, as she took in the scene. This was no longer a pleasant evening out. This— this was much more serious.

"Who on earth would do such a thing?" said Blackmarr, with an astonished look. "And why?"

"I don't know," said Vogel. "But I think the best thing is to get you away from here. I have a feeling they were after the formula, whoever they were."

48

"The formula, the formula," Blackmarr said, with irritation. "If this is what it's going to mean, I'd rather just destroy the thing."

Vogel sniffed the air and glanced toward the far end of the lab. A door stood open and a faint wisp of something trailed out. She raised her gun. "Professor, what's in there?" Vogel asked, indicating the door.

He turned to look. "My office."

"We've got smoke," said Davis.

"I know," she said, nodding to him. "Richard, you and the professor get behind me."

They did as she said, and Vogel approached the doorway on full alert. "If anyone is in there, I'm a government intelligence agent and I'm armed," she said to the smoke.

There was no response.

She craned her neck, then in one quick motion, kicked the door open and whipped inside. The gun pointed in front of her like an arrow. The source of the smoke was obvious. The professor's computer monitor had been smashed and the exposed wiring had started a small fire.

Vogel lowered her gun and looked around. The rest of the office had also been raided. Books and papers lay on the floor, along with drawers yanked from the desk.

"Good heavens," Blackmarr said, stepping inside. "My work, my experiments . . ."

Davis walked past him to the spot where the computer had stood. He blew out the fire and waved the smoke away. "They were looking for it," he said. "I'll bet you anything."

"Is the hard drive intact?" asked Vogel.

Davis stooped down and looked under the desk. "Vogel," he said after a moment. "You may want to look at this."

Vogel stepped around to where he was standing. "Oh, perfect."

The plastic tower that contained the computer's memory had been kicked over. A bullet hole neatly torn through its center.

Davis shook his head. "They didn't leave much, did they?"

"No, they didn't." Vogel turned to Blackmarr, who was still clutching his briefcase. "Professor, I know this is hard, but is this the only place you stored your work?"

He blinked as if he were coming out of a trance. "What?"

"The work on your discovery. Is there anywhere else you would have stored it? A backup, maybe? I need to know."

"The work was never stored there."

"It wasn't?"

"No. I was having difficulty with that machine and was afraid I would lose it. I kept all my findings on this." Blackmarr dug into the bag and produced a gray diskette.

"Nice," Davis said with a sigh. "Well, that's the end of that."

"No, it's not," said Vogel.

"What do you mean?"

"Whoever did this wasn't just looking for the formula. They were making a point. It's a warning."

An uneasy expression came over Davis' face. "What kind of warning?"

"They didn't get what they were after, so they'll be back."

The room suddenly grew silent, and it was Blackmarr who finally spoke. "Who will be back?"

Vogel further surveyed the damage. "I wish I knew."

* * *

Professor Simon Blackmarr leaned against the restroom wall and tried to catch his breath. He'd told the government woman he needed a moment, but he was actually scared to death.

What was happening?

A few hours ago, he'd been happily reviewing the periodic table with his evening class. Now his laboratory had been ransacked, his computer destroyed, and an intelligence agent was trying to pack him off to Washington to prevent his being killed by sinister forces. All because of a random accident, during a routine experiment.

Why couldn't he have just left well enough alone?

The harsh fluorescent light reflected off the green tile and Blackmarr swallowed. Panic clawing at him. Everything was spiraling out of control and he desperately wanted to just leave. Simply get in his car and drive off like any other day. Glancing at the mirror, he noticed his left hand was still clutching his briefcase. Unconsciously he had carried it inside with him. A wild thought flashed through his mind.

Why not?

It would be simple. Everything pertaining to his experiment was right here. The sample, the disc with his findings, even his notes from the lecture. Everything. If he acted quickly, he could get away and leave them with nothing.

It was an intoxicating idea, and the more he thought about it the better it sounded. His family owned property up north and he'd been meaning to take a sabbatical. There seemed no better time than right now. If he drove all night, he could reach the house by morning. Once there he would burn all of it, down to the smallest scrap of paper.

After a few weeks things would die down and then if this Vogel person came looking for information, he could honestly say there was none. It seemed ingeniously simple.

Blackmarr felt better. He set the briefcase on the counter and removed the small container he had shown Vogel earlier. There wasn't much time. They would be looking for him shortly.

* * *

Vogel stood beside Davis inside the lab and leaned against a table. Their hips touched. She re-engaged the safety on the automatic and reholstered it. Davis looked at her.

"What?" she asked.

"Nothing. I've just never seen you in action before. It's taking a little getting used to."

"We don't usually take civilians with us. But now that you've seen what I do, what do you think?"

"I think you're good," Davis said. "Very good."

A weak smile played across her face. "Thanks for sticking around," she said, her voice softening. "That was nice."

"I wouldn't have missed it. So, what happens now?"

Vogel shrugged. "Now I'll have to report it. Tell Twelve everything so they can investigate. Then take the professor and his research back to headquarters and write a lengthy report."

"Tonight?"

She looked at him and nodded. "Yeah, tonight." Something inside made her ask the next question. "Want to come?"

Davis grimaced. "I have a deadline."

She looked down. "That's sort of what I figured."

"I'm sorry, Lora."

"I understand."

They stood together for a moment, not speaking, and then she turned to him. Felt herself moving closer and closer until— Vogel, get it together. What are you doing?!

"Where's the professor?"

"What?" said Davis, somewhat surprised.

"The professor." "He said he was just going to the men's room. Where is he? It's been at least ten minutes."

* * *

Blackmarr stood at the bottom of the stairwell in front of the exit and looked up. When he was certain he was alone he retrieved the container from his briefcase and slid the cube back inside it. Immediately color returned to the world. Dropping the container into the bag he pushed the handle on the heavy door and stepped out onto the sidewalk.

The night air immediately felt crisp and cool on his face. Blackmarr breathed it in and sighed. Just being outside somehow made him feel much calmer and more at ease. He smiled again, then laughed out loud.

It had worked!

That government woman would eventually figure out what he had done and the two of them would roam around the building for hours trying to find him. Maybe his invention was good for something after all, getting out of difficult situations.

Blackmarr laughed again and tried to get his bearings. The exit had brought him out behind the building. Scanning the parking lot, he was surprised to see people still milling around. The lecture had been over for at least half an hour, although to him an entire evening seemed to have passed. Shrugging, he started in the direction of his car. He had only taken a few steps when he noticed two men approaching him. The one on the left was taller, with a sharp nose and angular chin. The other had stark white hair and a visible scar on his left cheek.

"Professor, Blackmarr," the tall one said, with a tight, predatory smile. "My associate and I enjoyed your lecture very much."

"Thank you."

"We were wondering if we could talk with you for just a moment?"

"I'm sorry, but I'm running rather late this evening," he said, attempting to keep moving. "If you'll excuse me."

The one with white hair grabbed his right shoulder, blocking his path. "I'm afraid we'll have to insist." With his other hand, he opened his coat, revealing a holstered gun.

Blackmarr's eyes widened, nervously. "Really, gentlemen?" he managed, "Is this entirely necessary?"

"I'm afraid it is," the dark-haired one said.

They began leading him gently, but firmly away, and he glanced reluctantly back at the exit.

"What is it you want?"

"Everything will be explained," the white-haired one told him.

* * *

Davis followed Vogel as she rushed from the lab into the men's restroom. She didn't announce herself.

A wadded paper towel lay on the floor and a small stream of water flowed from one of the faucets, but there was no sign of the professor.

"Damn!" Vogel said to the air.

"Maybe he went to a different one."

Vogel shook her head as she checked the stalls. All were empty.

"No, that wasn't the idea at all! I should have been paying attention."

"What do you mean?"

She glanced over in frustration. "Don't you see? He's got the thing on him and everything that goes with it. He's giving us the slip!"

Moving past him she charged back into the hallway. Davis grabbed the door handle, struggling to keep up.

"I don't need this right now," Vogel groaned, staring down the vacant corridor. "I really don't need this. I'm supposed to be on vacation."

Davis had begun putting the pieces together and turned to her. "You don't think he's actually using that thing, do you?'

"That's exactly what I think," said Vogel. "He wants us to play hide-and-seek with the invisible man, while he slips out through a side door somewhere and gets away."

"That's actually a pretty good plan. I remember trying to find classes in this place and it's no trick to get lost."

"Maybe so, but I still smell a rabbit."

"What does that mean?"

"Richard, the man still needs his car. Come on!"

* * *

Racing down the stairwell, Davis had a new respect for the woman in front of him. It was all starting to make sense now. He'd glimpsed this person before, but only briefly, and usually when she was telling a story. However, tonight, in the lab with the professor, he had finally seen Lora Chandler become Vogel, the high-level intelligence operative, and it had been astonishing. The singular action of drawing her gun, her body language, facial expressions, and even her speech had changed. The effect was undeniable.

He was attracted to her all over again.

They reached the bottom of the stairs and exited through the heavy metal door. It opened onto a sidewalk at the edge of the parking lot. A few cars remained scattered across it and Davis recognized his own beneath a light pole.

"He came out here," Vogel said, looking around. "I'll bet anything on it."

"I think you may be right," he said touching her arm. She looked at him and he nodded toward a black, unmarked van, some distance away. The side door was open and two figures were hurriedly forcing a third inside. "Tell me that's not what I think it is."

"Oh hell!"

"I don't think they're taking him for a joyride."

"No, they're not," Vogel yanked her gun from her purse and disengaged the safety. "Get the car."

"What are you going to do?"

"Just get the car," she said, pointing to the van.

* * *

Simon Blackmarr had never been kidnapped before. But that was what this was amounting to. There was absolutely no way out of this situation. Climbing into the van, he wondered if he would ever see the campus, or anything else again.

The man with the gun slid into the seat beside him and the door closed from the outside. Blackmarr leaned his head against the headrest and shut his eyes tightly. A mixture of dizziness and panic swept over him and for a moment he thought he would pass out. The van began to move and his panic changed to desperation, and finally to a kind of empty, numb feeling. He sighed.

Why in the world hadn't he simply stayed with that Vogel woman?

The trick had certainly worked. There was no chance of her possibly finding him now. No chance at all.

* * *

Vogel dashed across the parking lot, cursing herself for choosing boots. Her purse whacked into her side with each stride. She should have left it with Davis, but it contained her ID and mobile phone, and she would need both at some point.

Holding the gun in her left hand, she sprinted toward the van. As she approached, it began to move, making a wide arc toward the lot's rear exit. Vogel stopped. Her breath was coming in rapid bursts and sweat beaded on her forehead. There was no way to catch it, but if she could read the license plate, they could find out who was behind all of this.

It didn't work.

Other cars started moving across the lot and at the last minute, the van swung around and zoomed away in the opposite direction. Vogel made a last-ditch effort to chase it, but it was too late. The black vehicle vanished around the corner and was swallowed up in traffic.

"Hell," she repeated softly.

Vogel wiped her brow and reengaged the safety on the pistol. The sight of headlights and the sound of tires beside her caused her to stop and look over. Davis pulled alongside and lowered his window.

"What happened?"

Vogel jammed the gun back in her purse and glared at him. "They got away."

* * *

The van moved swiftly through traffic and finally merged onto the expressway. The professor watched through the side window, trying to make some mental note of where he was being taken. He had the wild thought of trying to overpower the gunman and seize control of the van. It worked on TV.

He sat back and attempted to think calmly. It was obvious they did not want to kill him. At least not right away. That could have been accomplished anywhere by now. They wanted to know what he knew. And they wanted his formula. But why? And who were they, for heaven's sake? That was the question he most wanted the answer to.

Blackmarr turned to the man with the gun and raised an irritated eyebrow.

"I suppose it would be the height of rudeness for me to ask where I'm being taken," he said.

"Not at all," he replied. "Mr. Malachai wants to speak with you. He's a great admirer of your work."

"Who the devil is Mr. Malachai?" Blackmarr asked. "And why didn't he simply call and make an appointment?"

"Mr. Malachai doesn't do things that way."

"So, he bundles people off in the middle of the night when he wants to see them? Is that it?"

The man gave him a slight smile. "We did ask you to come along on your own, professor. I really would have preferred it that way."

"And I would have preferred to have been left alone."

"I'm sorry but I can assure you Mr. Malachai will see that you're quite comfortable and well compensated for any inconvenience. He's a very hospitable host."

Blackmarr snorted and turned back to the road. Streetlights whizzed past but he could make out no discernible landmarks. "I don't suppose you have anything to drink in this prison."

"Of course, if you're willing to cooperate." He showed the gun beneath his coat again.

"You can stop displaying that obscene thing; I'm not going anywhere."

The man nodded and closed his coat. "Just as long as we both understand that I still have it."

"We understand."

"Very well." The man opened a panel in the rear of the passenger seat, revealing a small selection of bottles and glasses. "What would you like, professor?"

"Scotch. Two fingers"

The man poured two fingers' worth of a pale, brown liquid from one of the bottles and handed it to him. Blackmarr sipped it carefully. It was surprisingly good. In a different setting, he would have appreciated it for the distinct, smokey flavor with just a trace of vanilla. He took another sip and looked at his companion.

"Other people are looking for me, you know," he said.

"Yes, we know," the man replied smoothly. Blackmarr took a long sip of his drink, as the reality of his situation began to sink in.

Chapter 5

Twelve's image stared back from the portable computer with disapproval. Vogel sat at the bedroom table of the hotel suite, fidgeting as she looked at the screen.

"And you have no information at all?" Twelve repeated.

"It was a plain black van," Vogel said to the tiny, built-in camera. "I wasn't able to read the license plate." Bats flew in her stomach. This wasn't going well. She could feel Twelve's silent judgment growing, and every answer she gave just seemed to dig the hole deeper.

"You're to be prepared at all times, Vogel. Every assignment is important. Every one. I shouldn't have to tell you this."

"I understand." She swallowed hard. "What would you like me to do now?"

Twelve was silent for too long. An inscrutable expression on her face. "Nothing," she finally said.

Vogel blinked. "Nothing?"

"I'm going to have to review this with the Director of Operations. He'll need to determine exactly what we're dealing with before taking any action."

"But the man has been kidnapped. Shouldn't we at least alert local law enforcement? They may be able to at least provide some SA."

Twelve shook her head. "Involving the police may be exactly what they want, Vogel. If we're not careful, we could risk losing control of the whole situation."

Vogel started to protest but thought better of it.

"Stand by and I'll contact you as soon as I have further instructions."

"Understood."

"Out."

Twelve touched a key and the department logo appeared on the screen, ending the conversation. Vogel was irritated. She got up from the chair and walked into the next room of the hotel suite, where Davis was sitting on a small sofa. A bottle of beer sat on an end table, and he pretended to read a magazine.

"How did it go?" he asked, looking up.

"Weren't you listening?"

"Sort of."

"Then you know how it went," she said, dropping down next to him. "My boss just put me in time-out. I can't believe I actually let him go to the restroom by himself. I'm a professional agent, for heaven's sake. I'm supposed to know better than this."

"Is that really what she said?"

"Not in so many words."

"It was a calculated decision. You can't control what other people do. That's not your job."

"That's exactly my job. Or part of it at least."

"Vogel . . ."

"Richard, let me pout, all right? I'm in a really bad mood." She sighed and leaned her head against the back of the sofa.

Davis finished the beer and stood up.

"What are you doing?" she asked, looking at him.

"It's been a big day, and you're tired. I should go and let you get some rest."

"I'd rather you didn't."

Davis smiled. "Good night, Lora."

* * *

Richard Davis turned his car onto the highway and breathed a sigh of relief. What had just happened? This was supposed to have been an average evening with Cathy. A movie, a few drinks at the corner bar, and a walk on the beach.

Just like every Friday.

Instead, he'd gotten mixed up in whatever this was. He still wasn't sure. Something to do with the government and invisibility. There had been guns and Lora had gone into spy mode—which he admitted was incredibly attractive—but what did it all mean? Even she didn't seem to know.

Davis shook his head. He wasn't doing this. He wasn't getting involved with that woman again. Yes, she was cool, yes, she was charismatic, but she was also a serious loose cannon. Plus, she was wedded to her job and that would never change. It was the third wheel he would always be competing with, and it was too exhausting. Besides, she'd told him she couldn't get serious anyway. The best thing he could do was leave it alone. She'd probably be gone in the morning anyway.

Davis hit the turn signal and pulled into the Gateway Apartments complex. It was an uninspiring collection of two-story brick buildings with wrought-iron stairways. He parked in front of building D and shut off the engine. Getting out of the car he could already hear the roar of the ocean and smell the salt in the air. He immediately felt better. A quick walk on the beach to clear his head followed by a decent night's sleep. That was what he needed. Things would look differently in the morning.

Davis started down the sidewalk. He had nearly reached the entrance when a figure stepped out of the shadows.

"Richard Davis."

The voice was smooth, and the man approaching him was sharply dressed. His movements deliberate,

Davis stopped. "Yeah?"

"You spent the evening with the agent known as Vogel?"

"What?"

"Vogel. You're acquainted with her?" the man asked, stopping within an arm's reach. His hazel eyes, eerily sharp beneath his stark white hair,

"Hey, what is this?" asked Davis.

"Please answer the question."

"All right, I'm acquainted with her. And yes, we were together tonight. And if you're seeing her, I didn't know anything about it. We've been broken up for several months and I'm going out with someone else. It was just dinner."

The man managed a weak smile. "Interesting assumption. I have a message for her."

"You have a message for Vogel?"

"That's correct."

"So, use the phone." He started to move past, but the man grabbed him solidly by the shoulder. Davis turned to him, irritated. "Look, pal, I've had a long day and a very bizarre evening. I don't have any time for games."

The stranger's expression was serious as he leaned in. "I have a message for the woman, Vogel. Please listen."

Davis could feel the man's hot breath inches from his face, the pressure on his shoulder sharp and unforgiving. Pain flared through him, making it hard to think. "All right, all right! I'm listening!"

"Give us the disc."

"What?"

The man leaned in closer, his grip tightening. "Give us the disc, or there will be consequences."

The menace in the hazel eyes was unmistakable. Then, just as suddenly, the man released him, stepping back. "You'll be contacted soon."

Furious, Davis swung at the stranger, his fist connecting with a satisfying thud. He didn't see the left hook. Coming out of nowhere, it caught him squarely in the jaw. Davis staggered backward, as the world reeled, then crashed onto the asphalt.

* * *

Morning.

Vogel was awake, showered, and dressed. She was in the bathroom, sitting on the toilet lid, drinking the terrible coffee available in every hotel room in the world. In between sips, she smoked a cigarette. The exhaust fan carried the smoke to other parts of the hotel.

She shouldn't be doing this, she told herself.

Aside from the fact that it was a non-smoking room, she'd officially quit. Nevertheless, she kept a pack in her luggage for emergencies, and this was an emergency.

She'd had two drinks after Davis left, and then a third. Followed by a bath, where she'd listened to the entire Kill 'em All album, by Metallica, on her portable CD player. When she'd finally crawled into bed, sleep had been elusive. Leaving her to stare at the slow, hypnotic spin of the ceiling fan. Replaying every mistake, every misstep. She was an agent, damn it—why did everything feel so out of control? Perhaps there really was such a thing as a no-win situation. It was what she had originally thought about herself and Richard Davis. But now, maybe that analogy was incorrect.

There was a knock at the door. Vogel finished the cigarette, crushed it out, and flushed the end. Downing the last of the coffee, she checked herself in the mirror. Black pants, a white top, and a gray blazer. She didn't want to fool with hair, so she'd donned her fedora. She'd also traded the boots for a comfortable pair of black, department-issued oxfords. Her wallet and ID were tucked into an inside pocket and her gun was fastened under her left arm.

Today, she wouldn't be fooling with a purse.

Vogel walked to the door and put an eye to the peek hole. What she saw startled her. Davis stood outside in the hallway looking haggard. His hair was unkempt, and he was dressed in the same clothes as the day before. There was also a large bruise on his face. She immediately opened the door.

"Richard?"

Davis nodded at her. "We've gotta talk," he said, stepping inside.

"What on earth happened?" she said, closing the door. "Were you in a fight?"

"You could say that. I met one of your friends last night."

"What?"

"That's what I said. He was waiting outside my apartment. Told me to tell you that they want the disc and they're going to contact you about it. He said not cooperating would be a bad idea."

"Who was it? Did he say who he was with?"

"No. We didn't have a chance to exchange business cards."

"Well, why did you wait until now to tell me about it?"

"Because after he gave me the message, he knocked me out. I just woke up about an hour ago."

"Good grief!"

Davis sat down in a chair. "Lora, is this really the kind of stuff you deal with at work? Because if it is, I think I owe you an apology. I kind of thought you were exaggerating a bit."

"He knocked you out, just like that?" Vogel said, crouching down beside him.

"Well, I may have provoked him a little."

"What did you do?"

"I told him you and I had dinner. I think he may have had a thing for you."

The corners of her mouth turned up slightly and she cleaned grass from his hair. "Richard, I'm so sorry about this."

"Lora, these people aren't playing around, whoever they are. I think we should do something."

"We are going to do something," Vogel said, standing up. "I'm going to contact Twelve right now." She was turning toward the bedroom when there was a second knock at the door. The two of them exchanged glances.

"Did you order room service?" asked Davis.

"No."

"They may have followed me."

"Don't worry. I'm not going to let anything happen to you." She walked back to the door and peered through the peek hole a second time. "I don't believe it," she said, after a moment.

"Is it them?"

"No," Vogel said, looking over her shoulder. "It's Shade."

"What's Shade?"

"She's a 'spook.' Kaskarian Intelligence. I've worked with her before. I bet Twelve had them send her."

She opened the door and a slender woman with chestnut hair, in a charcoal pantsuit, stood just outside. The last time Vogel had seen her was in Venice.

"Shade," she said.

"Vogel."

"It's nice to see you."

"It's nice to see you, too." Her accent was slight and pleasant.

Vogel hesitated, then looked her in the eyes. "Can you tell me the color of Mrs. Weatherby's house?"

Shade raised an eyebrow, slightly and nodded. "White with blue trim and green shutters."

"And the name of her dog?"

"Alexander."

Vogel nodded. "Please come in." She stepped aside as Shade entered the room.

Davis immediately stood up.

"This is my friend, Richard Davis," said Vogel.

Davis waved.

"Hello," said Shade.

Vogel turned to her. "I suppose Twelve told you, we've had a little trouble over the past twenty-four hours."

"I know all about it," said Shade. "Vogel, you're both in extreme danger. I'm to take you to a safe location."

"What about him?" Vogel indicated Davis.

"Twelve is bringing both of you back to Washington to be debriefed."

"But he's a civilian. She didn't mention anything about that yesterday."

Shade seemed tense. "Vogel, your communication has been compromised. The agency has been trying to reach you for

72

several hours. Please, we don't have much time. Where is the disc?"

* * *

The car would have been appropriate for a head of state. It was long and black, with leather interior, and a tinted plexiglass shield that could be raised or lowered to provide privacy. Vogel sat next to Davis in the backseat. Shade sat opposite the two of them. If it had been yesterday evening, the arrangement might have seemed romantic. Under the circumstances, Vogel was just glad to be here. There was help now. She had worked with Shade before on other missions. She was a professional. It was possible they could resolve the situation before things went any further.

Vogel leaned forward. "Shade, what's going on? Who's behind all this?"

Shade started cautiously, "They're called Ion."

She shrugged. "I don't know that name. Are they new?"

"In a manner of speaking. They're also very old."

"How did TI find out about them?"

"I'm not at liberty to say."

Standard answer, thought Vogel. "What do they want?"

"Power, naturally."

"That's a little vague, isn't it?"

"Not necessarily."

"Are they working with anyone else?"

Shade looked at her but didn't answer. Vogel was about to repeat the question when Davis suddenly tapped her shoulder. "We're turning left."

"What?"

Davis pointed out the passenger window. "We just left the highway. This leads away from the city."

"What are you talking about?" Vogel leaned over and tried to look through the tinted glass.

"We're going the wrong way," said Davis. "There's nothing out here except open country.

Vogel's pulse quickened and her instincts began to fire as she turned back to Shade who was oddly silent. "Shade, what's going on?"

A peculiar expression had come over her face. "We told you, you would be contacted."

Chapter 6

Professor Blackmarr sat on a stiff, small sofa, in a tastefully appointed room. A kind of parlor. And waited.

Behind him hung a painting of the seashore. In front of him sat a coffee table shaped like an oval. Across the room, a television stood on a small, oak cabinet. The remote control sat beside him on the sofa. He'd switched the set on, stared blankly at the screen for several seconds, then switched it off again. He simply couldn't concentrate.

The room had no clock, but his watch told him it was nearly eleven-thirty, which meant he had been waiting for over an hour. The man who had shown him in had assured him he would return momentarily. Apparently, some moments were longer than others.

Blackmarr rubbed his eyes. He had no idea where he had been taken. On arriving last night, the white-haired man and his companion had hustled him through various doors and hallways. Blackmarr had glimpsed people in suits and thought he had seen a meeting taking place in one of the rooms.

But he couldn't be sure. Everything had happened so fast.

Something had been added to his drink. He was sure of this because as they were moving down one of the corridors, his legs suddenly felt heavy, and he could barely keep his eyes open. The next thing he knew he was waking up in an elegant room and a young man in a waistcoat and white gloves was standing beside his bed. His clothes had been cleaned and pressed and after a well-prepared breakfast, he had been given a tour of a modern laboratory. The individual giving the tour then presented him with the opportunity of a lifetime. The facilities were entirely at his disposal, including the staff. All of his worldly problems would be taken care of, and he would be free to pursue any type of research he desired. He simply needed to recreate his experiment here, so that the results could be studied.

He had turned it down, of course, but for the briefest of moments he had considered it. To study, simply study, without the burdens of money and career interfering. Who wouldn't be tempted? Shortly thereafter, a tall young man with a pleasant face in a tailored suit had deposited him here.

Wherever here was.

Blackmarr stood up. The sofa hurt his back. He walked to the narrow window again and looked out. The view was extremely limited. A bank of trees behind a small pool with an iron bench. Earlier he had seen a man in gray overalls doing something to the water, but he was no longer there. Blackmarr rubbed his chin. His impression was that there were several buildings linked together like a conference center. And that he was somewhere on the western end of the campus. He was basing this theory partially on the look of sunlight and shadows on the ground.

It wasn't hard to figure out what would happen next. They had tried the friendly approach and been turned down. The next time they would be more forceful. He had already been relieved of his briefcase, which contained his research, and even his sample. What was missing was the knowledge of how to do it themselves. How to create the damn thing. Which is why they needed him in the first place. And this was what truly worried him.He didn't know how to do it.

On several different occasions, he had tried to duplicate his experiment. All had failed to produce satisfactory results. Something unusual had happened that particular day in the lab, which he was at a loss to fully explain. Even analyzing the sample didn't help. The very nature of the material itself prevented a conclusive reading.

They weren't going to believe this, and he knew it. They were going to want results and when he was unable to give them any they were going to—

The door opened suddenly. Blackmarr looked over his shoulder to see the young man in the tailored suit pushing a small cart into the room. On it was a tray of food.

"My apologies, professor," he smiled. "I didn't intend to be gone quite so long."

Blackmarr studied the tray. There were toasted bagels, an assortment of fruit, muffins, and fresh coffee. The heavy aroma filled the air like perfume.

"I've already had breakfast," he said, wanting a cup.

"Well, we thought you could use a refresher. Also, I have some good news for you. You'll soon have some help."

* * *

The long car paused as a pair of iron gates opened electronically, Vogel looked through the window. The estate was huge and seemed to extend in all directions. They continued along a curving road, toward a massive house. One that, in Vogel's opinion, could have passed for a palace in several countries.

A group of men in dark suits were waiting as they pulled up to the main entrance. Doors were opened and the three of them were escorted out and into the house. Inside the foyer, Vogel and Davis were checked for weapons. Vogel

78

surrendered her gun to a man with a flat nose and a blank expression.

"I'll be needing that back when I leave," she said, flatly.

The remark produced no reaction from the flat-nosed man, who merely walked away. A moment later a butler appeared and led the three of them into a room with thick carpeting and an elaborate oak desk. The butler nodded silently in their direction, then disappeared through a set of double doors. The three of them stared at one another.

"What's all this about?" Davis whispered.

"I haven't the foggiest," hissed Vogel.

"Shhhh," said Shade.

Vogel glanced around, casually studying the decor. It was tasteful without being stuffy, which was always a balancing act. The grandfather clock was an especially nice touch. She would have picked a different painting, however. Something with more yellow.

One of the double doors reopened and a heavy-set man entered the room. Vogel gauged him to be roughly in his mid-fifties. His hair was gray and thinning and a carefully trimmed beard occupied most of his face. He held a cigar in his left hand and paused before slowly making his way to the desk. The three of them watched in silence.

The man took a sheet of paper from the desk and absently puffed his cigar. He studied the page as he sat down in the leather chair. Shade politely cleared her throat.

"Agent Vogel and Mr. Richard Davis to see you," she said.

"That will be all," said the man, without looking up.

Shade nodded and silently exited. The man lowered the paper and studied it carefully. His eyes came to rest on Davis.

"You are not needed," he said.

Some sort of signal was given, and, in a moment, two men entered and began leading Davis out.

"Wait, what's going on, where are you taking me?!" he protested loudly. "Vogel, what are they doing . . ."

Stunned, she watched as the two men carried him by the arms into the hallway. The heavy doors slammed shut and Richard Davis was suddenly gone.

Vogel spun around and stared at the bearded man, who had been observing everything with indifference. She started to speak, but he cut her off.

"You'll forgive me for being somewhat dramatic," the man said, "but I felt this was a conversation we should hold in private." He placed the cigar in an ornate ashtray and looked at her. "Agent Vogel, also known as Lora Chandler. We meet at last."

"Who are you?" said Vogel.

"My name is Malachai."

"As in, the prophet?"

Malachai raised an eyebrow. "Very good. You know your scripture."

"I went to Sunday school."

"Then you know Malachai brought a message of warning to the priests, for failing to uphold God's commandments."

"It sounds familiar."

"Good. Then I'll spare you the preamble. I'm sure you have a number of questions."

"Yes, I do. For starters, what is this all about, and why have you kidnapped Simon Blackmarr?"

"Direct and to the point," Malachai said, slowly standing up. "I like that. Vogel, as a representative of the United States government, I'm sure you're aware of the confused mess it's currently in."

"It has some problems, yes."

"Some problems? That's a diplomatic way of putting it." He picked up his cigar and held it between two fingers. "It also appears to be a running theme. Point to any spot on the globe and I defy you to find a government that's not riddled with hypocrisy, corruption, and inefficiency. World leaders strut around, beating their chests, while their people go hungry. They argue over lines on a map while the poor huddle in doorways. They pass laws that mean nothing and close their ears while drug use skyrockets, crime runs rampant, and the young and the old suffer. But that's all about to change. And you're going to be part of it, Vogel."

"That's an interesting way to begin a conversation," she said. "How exactly?"

Malachai began walking around the desk, making his way to where she stood. "I trust you have the information?"

"If you mean the disc with the professor's notes, then yes."

"Wonderful! This should solve things nicely. Blackmarr is a talented man, but he does have his flaws." He held out a hand to Vogel. "May I have it, please?"

She paused. "And if I say 'no'?"

Malachai winced. "Yes, well, that would be rather unfortunate. Let's keep things on a pleasant note, shall we?"

Vogel removed the disc from her inside coat pocket. She handed it to Malachai, who immediately smiled. "Thank you so much. The poor man is convinced I'm going to kill him. This will ease his mind considerably."

Another signal was given, and the door opened a third time. The butler returned and strode across the carpet. "See that this is delivered to the professor at once, please," Malachai said, passing him the disc.

"Yes sir." He accepted it in a white-gloved hand and swiftly exited.

Vogel watched and furrowed her brow. Her instincts told her that some sort of wireless technology was being employed to signal the servants. But she'd be damned if she could figure out what it was.

"Now, where was I?" said Malachai.

"You were explaining who you represent and how you intend to use the professor's invention to save the world," said Vogel. "Or words to that effect."

The corners of Malachai's beard turned up and he drew on his cigar, exhaling a long plume of smoke. "I suppose it does sound farfetched. But we aren't doing anything that shouldn't have been done long ago."

"And just who are we, Mr. Malachai? You keep dodging the question."

Malachai shifted his weight. "Why don't we sit down?" he said, leading her to a pair of overstuffed chairs. "Let's say we're a network of sorts," he said, folding himself into one. "A cooperative of well-placed individuals who feel there's a better way."

Vogel sat down opposite him. "And what is this better way?"

"For starters, the removal of boundaries and the eliminating of unnecessary burdens."

"Such as?"

"Lines on a map, for example."

"You mean countries."

Malachai smiled. "Names mankind has invented. They don't exist in any real sense. The Internet is already erasing these invisible barriers."

Vogel was growing irritable. This was taking too long, and she wanted a cigarette. Leaning forward in her chair she locked eyes with the heavyset man. "Malachai, I am, by nature, blunt. I think this conversation might go better if you kept that in mind. Now, why don't you tell me just what in the hell you're proposing?"

Malachai removed the cigar from his mouth. He was silent for a moment and when he spoke again his face was darker. "Very well," he said. "The people of the earth need help. Food is hoarded on one side while starvation takes place on the other. Money and education are wasted by the privileged while others live in ignorance and squalor. Governments do nothing but argue and make war. We intend to abolish this way of thinking and implement a new system."

"What kind of system?"

"An empire."

Vogel's eyes grew wider. "With you as the emperor, I suppose?"

He nodded. "Precisely."

Vogel's breath hitched, a cold shiver running down her spine as her heart raced. He's crazy, she thought. Mad as a hatter. This was the stuff of comic books and Saturday morning cartoons. And yet there he was, in full color, actually saying it—and worse, believing it. She didn't know whether to laugh or call for a straitjacket. "And just how do you intend to institute something like that?"

His eyes were fixated on her. "Something will happen that will get the attention of the world. Like a star falling from the heavens. After this, there will be an announcement made at the Conference of

Nations. It won't be taken seriously. Then a certain world leader will be eliminated, throwing that country into chaos. Another will follow, and perhaps another. The pattern will continue until an emergency meeting is called, at which time, another announcement will be made. More forcefully. By then, the conference will have no choice but to concede."

"And why is that?" Vogel said. She suspected she already knew the answer.

"Because Miss Chandler. One cannot defeat one's opponent if one cannot see them."

* * *

Vogel perched on the edge of the bed, scanning the room. It was tastefully decorated, almost soothing. A small couch and ottoman sat across from her, along with an end table. Sconce lamps were built into the wall and a painting of a deer in an autumn forest hung between them. She even had a small bathroom and a tiny coat closet. It reminded her of a suite in an upscale hotel. And if not for the fact that it was her prison, she might have enjoyed it. That, however, was a large point of contention.

She had been led to the room shortly after her conversation with Malachai by a young man with a yellow tie. He could not have been more than twenty-three years old. Vogel had tried talking to him, but he made no response. Aside from Malachai, no one here seemed to speak. The man had deposited her here, then quickly left.

Vogel crossed her legs and looked at the painting again. Her stomach rumbled loudly. The last thing she'd eaten had been the manicotti at the Italian restaurant with Richard. A year ago, it seemed. She tried to ignore the hollow feeling and focus on the problem at hand.

How to get out.

The door suddenly opened, and she looked up. The young man with the yellow tie entered, carrying a tray. Vogel nodded at him.

"Couldn't stay away, huh? My charm was just too intoxicating."

The young man stared at her blankly.

"Okay, maybe not."

He set the tray down carefully on the ottoman.

"You know, as long as you're here, I could use a drink. Double bourbon, neat."

The man with the tie paused, gave her a confused look, and walked out wordlessly. The door clicking solidly behind him.

"I need better material," said Vogel. She got up and inspected the tray. It contained a meal. Roasted chicken breast on a brioche bun, with lettuce and tomato. A baked potato with tiny butter and salt packets, along with a high-end bottle of water. For dessert, a slice of cheesecake had been provided, drizzled with raspberry sauce. Vogel noted appreciatively that the plates and dinnerware were plastic, but the napkin was cloth.

Pulling the ottoman closer to the small sofa, she sat down and began to eat.

* * *

Richard Davis picked up the lukewarm hamburger from the plastic plate and glanced at the locked door. A few moments ago, a center panel had dropped down and a metal tray had been pushed through. The tray held a hamburger, potato chips, and a can of soda. When Davis picked up the tray the panel had snapped back into place. There was nothing on his side of the door to reopen it.

He took a bite of the hamburger. It was tasteless. Meat and bun, without mustard or ketchup. Davis swallowed and took another bite. The holding cell—or whatever—was small, and consisted of bare white walls, a cheap wooden chair, and a narrow cot. The two men who had dragged him away from Vogel had all but flung him in here without a word of explanation. Since then, he had sat, paced, and stared at the ceiling for hours it seemed. All to no avail.

What did these people want?

He was a newspaper reporter, for heaven's sake. With a few phone calls and a well-placed story, he could expose whatever was going on here in no time. They were taking an enormous risk.

Davis munched a cold French fry. Maybe that was it, he thought. Maybe the reason they'd locked him in here was because he was a reporter and they saw him as a threat. He'd seen too much. Knew too much. It had happened before. Journalists asking questions they shouldn't, then disappearing without a trace. Davis felt an uncomfortable chill and drank soda from the can.

Except that he hadn't been asking questions. All he'd done was tag after Vogel like a puppy. She was the one who'd been taking notes. He was merely collateral. But they were never going to believe that. And even if they did, it wasn't likely that they'd risk simply turning him loose.

The thought sobered him.

Davis swallowed a fry and thought of Vogel. What had they done with her? Where was she? Was she still alive? Granted, Lora was a professional intelligence agent, but that didn't mean very much if they'd taken her weapons. For all he knew she could be dead now. A sinking feeling came over him as he began to grasp the reality of his situation. This was serious.

Glancing down at his plate he noticed something. It was sticking out from the left side, almost imperceptible. He picked his plate up and moved it aside. A small piece of cream-colored paper, folded in half, lay underneath the tray. Davis stared at it for a moment, then carefully picked it up.

* * *

Vogel set her empty plate aside and slipped off her left shoe. She removed the insole, and feeling inside, located a small button and pressed it. The heel suddenly dropped to the carpet. Vogel picked up the heel and removed a thin piece of serrated wire from the hollow. Snapping the heel back in place, she replaced the shoe and walked over to the closet.

A light switched on as she stepped inside. Below the ceiling sat a shelf, containing an extra pillow, and below this a wooden pole ran between the two walls-apparently for hanging clothes. Vogel studied the pole for a moment, then unwound the wire and slipped it over the center. Fitting the two loops on either end of the wire over her thumbs, she carefully began to saw.

* * *

Malachai sat at his desk and dined on cold pheasant and white wine. After dinner, he would have a cup of coffee and a slice of chocolate cake. His favorite. Taking a fresh bite, he thought about the plan again, running over the various scenarios in his head to ensure it was sound. He felt that it was, and the other members had agreed with him on this point. Of course, it was impossible to anticipate every contingency, but its strength lay in the fact that it was entirely new and therefore would catch the opposition unprepared. No one in history had ever attempted something quite like this. Nor been able to. And that was their greatest advantage. He hoped their objective could be accomplished with the least number of tragedies. In his heart, Malachai didn't care for violence.

This was one of the things he hoped to address. There was too much violence in the world now, and so much of it unnecessary. Under his leadership, violence would become scarce. People would respect one another. There would be a different court system. He already had it mapped out. In the new regime . . . but he was getting ahead of himself.

One step at a time.

Malachai sipped his wine and thought about the evening's events. Originally, this was to have been a small operation. Instead, it had become both complicated and time-consuming. There had been miscalculations on all sides. He had not anticipated the government woman, for one thing. Although, in hindsight, perhaps he should have. It only made sense. The question now was what to do about her. His first impression of Agent Vogel was that she was both capable and intelligent. This intrigued him, and in another setting, he would consider asking her to join the organization. Unfortunately, that was not possible now.

Eliminating her may—or may not—raise suspicions. Intelligence agents were eliminated all the time. It was a risk one accepted as part of the job. On the other hand, letting her go would be absolutely disastrous. Then again, if she were discovered, apparently intoxicated, or returned with false information, she would presumably become ineffective. Presumably. And that was a problem because they could never be entirely certain. Shade had been a much simpler matter.

Malachai finished the pheasant and took a bite of potato. Davis, on the other hand, was the proverbial fly in the ointment. No amount of foresight could have predicted a boyfriend reporter. True, he had little information, but this fact did not make him any less of a threat. As the saying goes, few things were as dangerous as the inspired amateur. This would require careful thought and a considerable amount of tact. And, perhaps, a large body of water.

* * *

Vogel was sweating. She was not a carpenter and whoever thought this concept up had obviously never tried it. But it was all she had to work with. The wooden bar was as solid as granite and each pass she made with the wire felt as if it was cutting into her hand. She swore under her breath, certain that blisters were forming on her palms. Nevertheless, she kept at it. Finally, something snapped, and a section fell to the floor. Vogel crouched down and picked it up, her hands stinging. The piece was roughly a foot long and two inches in diameter. It would do.

Vogel leaned the pole carefully against the inside wall and stepped out of the closet. Crossing the floor, she entered the small bathroom and turned on the hot water in the tiny shower. She waited until she saw steam rising and then exited the bathroom, leaving the door slightly ajar.

Returning to the closet, Vogel stood on her tiptoes and grasped the edges of the small, automated light. With one swift motion, she yanked it free. The closet grew dark, and Vogel closed the door until only a sliver of light remained. Grasping the pole in one hand, she put her eye to the thin crack of light and steadied herself. There was nothing to do now, she thought, drawing a deep breath, but wait.

* * *

Richard Davis read the note several times, then put it down. It was obviously a joke. And not a very good one.

BE READY

That was all it said, the letters scribbled in blue pen.

Ready? Ready for what?

An interrogation?

His own execution?

What?

It made no sense.

His mind raced with possibilities, each more paranoid than the last. There was nothing to do in the tiny room and he wanted some answers. Straighten things out. Clear the air. He wanted to talk to that guy with the beard, whatever his name was. Explain that the whole thing was a mistake and that whatever he might think, he wasn't working with Vogel. Mainly, he wanted out.

* * *

The closet was cramped, and Vogel could hear the sound of her own breathing.

She continued to stare through the thin crack of light with an unblinking eye. A moment later, she heard the door to her suite open, then close again. Her field of vision was limited, but she saw a shape move past the closet, then pause and enter the bathroom. Just as you should, she thought. The seconds crawled by, then, carefully opening the door, she stepped from the closet. The light momentarily blinded her. Vogel held the pole like a weapon, and as her eyes refocused, saw the back of a figure peeking into the bathroom.

She hadn't expected a woman.

Raising the bar like a baseball bat, she swallowed, her pulse quickening as she crept forward. The floor creaked, and in an instant, the figure spun around. Vogel froze and the woman's eyes went wide.

"Vogel, please, no!"

"Shade?"

The weapon slipped from Vogel's grip before she could stop herself. It was her face—there was no mistaking it. For a moment, she simply stared in shock. Then, fury raced through her. In an instant, she grabbed Shade by the shoulders and slammed her against the wall. "I should snap your neck!" Vogel snarled, her thumb pressing hard against the woman's windpipe. "What the hell are you doing mixed up in this?!"

"It's not what you think!" Shade gasped. Her eyes bulged from their sockets.

"I'll bet. How much are they paying you to turn traitor? Or maybe he's going to marry you and the two of you divide up the globe, huh?"

"You don't understand," her voice cracked. "You've got it all wrong—I swear!"

Vogel caught herself. She wasn't a murderer, and this wasn't a life-threatening situation. She released her thumb and Shade collapsed to her knees, gasping for breath. Vogel loomed over her, eyes still burning. "All right let's hear it," she demanded. "And make it good."

Chapter 7

Two years earlier

Doesha Shantowe, a.k.a. "Agent Shade," looked in the hotel mirror steadying her breath as she applied her lipstick with precision. Each movement was calculated— every detail had to be perfect. She studied her earrings, touched her hair with a brush, and nodded.

The dress worked.

It gave just the right note of elegance without calling too much attention to itself. Which is what she wanted. She should appear nondescript. Simply another face at an elegant party. The assignment itself was much more complex. Her target was a man about whom much was suspected, and little known. A man calling himself Malachai.

He was an international figure, whose origins were something of a mystery. A man of great wealth, apparent power, and influence, and he was rumored to have been connected to numerous suspicious incidents over the past several years. One involved trying to devalue the currencies of several countries.

Yet, there was no proof.

Nothing could be verified. Each trail ended in smoke. Kaskarian intelligence wanted her to find out exactly who he was and what he knew. And to do so without raising suspicion.

Shade had been cautiously trailing him for several days and, so far, had avoided being made. Tonight, she hoped to make actual contact. It was a gala event at an upscale hotel. Invitation only. Shade tucked a small pistol into her evening bag and gave herself a final once-over in the mirror. Break a leg, kid.

* * *

The car stopped at the hotel entrance and a doorman helped her out. That night her contact was a man named Sommersby, a member of Malachai's inner circle. Shade had carefully cultivated a relationship with him, on the pretext that she was interested in entering society. Sommersby had mentioned Malachai's name in passing and Shade let it drop that she would enjoy a meeting with such a fascinating person. He promised to arrange one.

Inside the hotel, Shade handed her invitation to a gloved man in a tuxedo. "Welcome, Miss Kasper," said the man. "We're delighted to have you this evening."

"Thank you," said Shade.

The man in the tuxedo led her to a ballroom, where she immediately spotted Sommersby. He stood near a small table, drinking Champagne and looking stiff. Sommersby was thin, with over-combed blond hair and eyes that were too close together. Shade felt he had the personality of a dishrag but pretended to be excited to see him and kissed him on the cheek.

"I was afraid you might not come," said Somemersby.

"Why would you think that?"

"You didn't phone."

"I'm sorry," said Shade, warmly. "I had so many things to do."

Sommersby seemed placated and offered a tight smile. "Would you care for a drink?"

"I'd love one."

* * *

The room spoke of money and prestige. An orchestra played classical music as evening gowns danced and flirted with tailored suits, as much for the sake of being seen as anything else.

Shade carried herself with ease and sophistication. She'd been at affairs like this before and held her glass like a lady as Sommersby led her across the room to the man she'd been observing. He was talking animatedly to a short, round man with fiery red hair. The expression on the red-headed man's face vacillated between astonishment and sheer terror.

Malachai stabbed the air with his finger as he spoke, and Shade noticed that he enjoyed commanding whatever space he occupied. He also had excellent taste in clothing. Sommersby waited for an opportune moment before interrupting.

"Sir," he said, as he laughed loudly. "Sir, this is the woman I wanted to introduce you to."

Malachai turned, mildly irritated. "What?" he said, noticing them. "Oh, yes, indeed!" Shade nodded and his smile widened. "Yes, this is the fascinating woman I've been hearing so much about. Miss . . . Kasper, is it not?"

"Cheryl," Shade said, offering her hand.

"Miss Cheryl Kasper," he said, taking it between two paws. "Delighted to meet you. I'm called Malachai."

"Thank you," said Shade.

Malachai made a dismissive signal with his left hand and Sommersby vanished.

"An interesting name," said Shade. "Is it your first or last?"

"It serves as both," he said, leading her to a sofa. "I'm told you're eager to meet me. How can I be of service to you this evening?" He waited for her to be seated before lowering himself into a chair across from her.

"I'm always eager to meet interesting people."

"Am I an interesting person, Miss Kasper?"

"You are to Mister Sommersby. He practically insisted I see you."

"That may be the most sensible thing he's done in a long time," Malachai said, playfully.

Shade smiled demurely and placed her hands in her lap. "I understand you're a patron of the arts, Mr. Malachai."

"I am, indeed, Miss Kasper."

"Please, call me Cheryl."

"Of course. Yes, Cheryl, I'm passionate about the theater."

"I wish to stage a private production of Macbeth at the Gray Theater. We'll need a director. Am I correct in assuming you'd be interested?"

Malachai beamed. "Miss Kasper, nothing would give me greater pleasure . . ."

"Cheryl."

"Cheryl. Dear Cheryl, nothing would give me greater pleasure. I bow to the bust of Shakespeare. Ever since my own debut as Hamlet in college. I'd be honored to be a part of your production."

Just as you should, thought Shade. "Wonderful," she said. "I'm truly thrilled."

"As am I." He stood up. "Now, enough business. The night is young, and we're in this lovely setting. Will you do the honor of allowing me to dance with you?" He put out his hand.

Shade put on her best smile as she took it. Inside she fumed. If she had been a man they would likely still be talking shop. She stood up gracefully and even managed to toss her hair. "It would be my pleasure," she cooed.

* * *

In a booth somewhere in the venue, Shade sat with Malachai, speaking softly. It was late and only a handful of guests remained. Malachai was drinking bourbon and lecturing. Shade had quietly switched to club soda and was listening intently, making mental notes. The subject was world affairs.

"Politics is for fools, my dear Cheryl," Malachai growled.

"Is it?"

"It always has been. The game of the wealthy and the corrupt. A blind man could see it in an instant."

"I suppose so."

"That's why something must be done. A change, a real change must descend upon this globe if it's to be fit to live on."

"What kind of change?"

"The kind that lasts."

A waiter appeared with two more drinks and Malachai nodded. "Ahh, we're rescued. I was becoming parched."

The waiter set the drinks in front of them and retreated.

Malachai looked at Shade carefully. "It's late, dear Cheryl, and I fear I'm boring you."

"Nonsense. I'm having a wonderful time."

Malachai picked up his glass. "Then a toast. To our new friendship. May it be long-lasting."

Shade picked up the glass of club soda. "Indeed," she said. She took a long sip and noticed Malachai watching her with interest.

She started to speak but there was an odd sensation in the back of her throat, and her mouth felt funny. Her eyelids suddenly felt odd, too. Incredibly heavy, as if keeping them open required enormous effort. Shade put a hand to her forehead. Trying to focus on what it was she wanted to say. Color seemed to drain from everything around her and she looked at Malachai, who was somehow very far away. He said something, but the words made no sense.

In a forced motion, she pushed herself from the table and tried to stand. Her head felt as though she were wading through thick fog. Voices whispered in her ears, and the world suddenly spun and went black.

* * *

She was awake.

The clock on the nightstand told her it was nine-thirty in the morning. She breathed deeply, rubbed her eyes a second time, and blinked. Where was she? She turned her head and saw that she was lying in a bed, in a very nice room. Maybe a hotel. The curtains had been partially drawn and sunlight streamed through the window.

Was this a friend's house?

Was it her house?

She didn't know. Everything was a blur, the world around her soft at the edges.

The door opened and a man with a beard came in, followed by another man in a tailcoat, carrying a tray of food.

"Good morning," said the man with the beard. "How are you feeling today?"

She stretched and sat up slowly as the tray was placed in front of her. "I'm not sure. I feel kind of . . ."

"Confused?" the man finished for her.

She nodded.

"I can understand that. You've had a rather interesting time of it."

A third man came in. He wore a white coat and carried a black bag.

She turned to the man with the beard. "Where am I?"

"Before I answer that, I'd like this gentleman to take a look at you. He's a physician."

"Why do I need a doctor?"

"We'll explain that as well. Dr. Nicholas, if you would."

The man in the white coat had very little hair and peered over his glasses with a neutral expression. He shined a light into her eyes, listened to her heart, and carefully touched the back of her head.

She winced. "Ouch!"

"Is that tender?" asked the physician.

"Yes."

"I'm not surprised. You got it pretty good back there."

"What's all this about?"

"Just a moment." He made notes in a black book, then looked at her. "What's the last thing you remember?"

"I . . ." She thought. But there was nothing there. "I don't know."

"Let's try something more basic. Can you tell me your name?"

She closed her eyes, then opened them again. Still nothing. "I'm . . . not sure."

"Mmm hmm." The man wrote more in the book. "Do you know who the current president is?"

Fog.

"No."

"Last question. Can you tell me what year it is?"

A slow panic was beginning to build in her stomach, and she looked at the man and shook her head.

The doctor closed the book and motioned to the man with the beard. The two of them stepped away from the bed and spoke in low voices, with their backs turned. She tried to listen but heard only mumbling. Finally, the bearded man turned around and came over to the side of the bed.

"I'm very sorry," he said. "But I'm afraid it was necessary. We wanted to make sure there were no complications."

Complications? She was nervous now. "What is this? What's going on? Where am I?"

"Try to relax. We'll take things one at a time. My name is Malachai. You're in my estate. This is one of my guest rooms."

"What am I doing here?"

"Two nights ago, you managed to enter the estate. It was late, and you were very confused. We think you may have taken something. We tried to help you, but you fought us and fell and hit your head on the outside stairs. Do you remember?"

She shook her head again.

"No, of course not. As I said, you seemed to have taken something. Dr. Nicholas and I managed to sedate you and clean you up. Then we put you to bed. You've been here ever since."

She blinked slowly, processing. "You said two nights. I've been here that long?"

"Yes. Most of the time you've been asleep."

Her stomach felt funny, and she stared at the bedspread. "You said I'd taken something. Do you mean drugs? Was I on drugs?"

The man hesitated. "It would appear so."

"What kind?"

"Well . . . let's just say it isn't anything you'd want to repeat."

She swallowed. "Can I ask a question?"

"As many as you like."

"Who am I?"

Malachai took a deep breath. "I'm afraid that's still to be determined."

"What do you mean?"

"Well, it seems you didn't have any identification. We're doing our best to find out but right now, since you're unable to identify yourself, we simply don't know."

She looked at the bedspread again. "Oh."

"Once we learn something, we'll inform you immediately. I promise."

An idea was starting to form in her mind, and she didn't like it. "You said I came here late, and I was on drugs."

"Yes."

"Why?"

"You were looking for help, apparently."

"What kind of help?"

"Well . . ." The bearded man looked uncomfortable.

"What?"

"Putting it rather delicately, you appeared to be indigent."

"Indigent?"

"A vagrant."

"A vagrant," she repeated. "You mean homeless. You're trying to tell me that I'm homeless, is that it?"

He had no response, and she swiped the covers back and started to get up.

"Wait a moment," the man put out a hand. "What are you doing?

"Thanks for the help. I'll get out of your house now."

"There's no need for that. At least give us the chance to help you determine who you are and recover. After all, this is partially our fault."

"You've done enough." She put a foot on the floor and suddenly felt lightheaded. The spot behind her ear stung again. "Oww."

"There now, see? You need to regain your strength. Our chef has prepared an excellent breakfast. Why don't you take some time, enjoy it, then get dressed? Afterward, we can talk again. Maybe some of the fogginess will have lifted."

She turned back to the tray. There were pancakes, eggs, bacon, orange juice, and coffee. The smells made her mouth water. Suddenly she wanted all of it.

* * *

The shower felt wonderful. She had no idea when she'd taken one last, but from what the man had said—if she was homeless—it could have been a long time. She tried not to think about that part. The shampoo felt nice in her hair and the hot water, cascading over her, seemed to wash away the confusion. If only for a moment.

Drying off, she noticed bruises on her shoulder. There was also a long white scar on her forearm. Where had that come from? She studied it. It seemed to have been made by a blade. Had she been in a fight? The questions continued to tumble and swirl.

A robe had been laid out for her on the bed. She slipped it on, feeling the warmth and softness, and looked into the mirror. It was as though she were staring at a stranger. Not a hint of recognition. The woman with the chestnut hair could just as easily have been someone sitting across from her on a bus.

She moved closer and inspected her features.

Whoever she was, she wasn't bad looking. It was a good face, with intelligent eyes, and an attractive figure. How in the world had she wound up on the street? Whatever had happened, it must have been earth-shattering.

* * *

The door opened as she was making up
the bed. She was fully dressed now and
glanced over her shoulder while smoothing
the bedspread. She needed something—
anything—to feel normal again, even if just
for a moment.

"There's no need for that," Malachai
said, stepping into the room. "We have
servants for this very thing."

"I like to pay my own way," she said.
"Besides, I've taken up enough of your time."

Malachai frowned. "You're leaving us
then?"

"I shouldn't stay, and from what you've
said, I've already caused enough trouble."

"I see." He stroked his beard and took a
few steps toward her. "Of course, it's your
decision, but have you thought about where
you'd go?"

She shrugged. "I suppose there are
places for people . . . in my situation."

"I suppose. But you came to us with no
identification and no money. How will you
support yourself?"

She hadn't thought about that. "It's not
your concern," she said, turning back to fluff
the pillows.

"It is my concern. A person arrives at my
home, confused, in need of assistance, with
no idea of who she is, no identification, and

no currency. You expect me to send such a person back out into the world alone? I won't hear of it."

"I can take care of myself."

"Perhaps, if you knew who you were. But just imagine if a police officer were to stop you. It's quite likely you'd wind up in jail. Is that really what you want?"

She frowned. "I appreciate what you're trying to do," she said, facing him, "but it's not necessary. I'm not interested in being a charity case."

"That's understandable. No one wants to be a burden. Would you feel better about the situation if you had a job?"

"A job?" She raised an eyebrow, curiously.

"Yes, a job."

"What kind of job?"

* * *

It was November.

Six months had passed since she'd first awakened at the estate. Jennifer—that was the name she'd chosen for herself—waited in the hall, outside the study. She'd sat in on many of Malachai's meetings, but this one was private. That was okay. From what he'd told her, it was also extremely important. Each of the key members of Ion was present and when it was finished, the last of the details of The Plan would be ironed out.

Malachai was wonderful. Brilliant, powerful, and devoted to the concerns and needs of others. This plan he spoke of would wipe away want and poverty forever and transform the world into a paradise. It was breathtaking. Each time he talked with her about it, a chill ran up her spine. Just to be around such a man was exciting and made her feel special. Needed.

Important.

In the short time she'd been involved, she'd made some contributions to the work, but they weren't nearly as significant as he claimed. Still, it was nice to feel appreciated and trusted. To feel as though she belonged. Her previous life was still a blank slate, but from what Malachai had told her, perhaps it was better not to remember. It had been harsh and brutal. A life of stark survival. This one was much better. If she never remembered her past, it wouldn't matter now. She'd traded a stone for a pearl.

Jennifer crossed her arms and smiled. He was going to be in there most of the evening.

They would have to postpone their walk. Perhaps she would go by herself a little later. She strolled casually down the hall, not thinking about anything in particular. The estate was quiet. Dinner had been held early and most of the servants had retired for the night.

He had wanted it that way.

The quiet seemed odd. Usually, the estate was humming with activity—bustling, even. She turned a corner and realized she'd wandered into the southern portion of the house. She didn't usually spend time here. It was primarily for guests. It was also where she had been taken, and opened her eyes the first day. She didn't like to think about that.

Now, however, as she walked along the thick carpet, she found herself in front of the very door to her old room. She stopped and stared. It didn't seem so imposing now. In fact, it looked very much like any other door. Jennifer put her hand out and touched the knob. Nothing happened. It felt cold and metallic in her hand, but that was all.

Cautiously, she turned it and to her surprise, the door opened. Usually, these rooms were locked when not in use. Apparently, someone forgot to check. Jennifer paused. It was unlikely the cameras would be turned on, especially now. She pushed the door open and stepped inside.

The room was dark.

Her hand found the wall switch and flipped it on. It seemed smaller than she remembered. And in all honesty, not especially unique. The truth was, if she'd not remembered the number, she would likely not have been able to recognize it. The bed and furniture were indistinguishable from the others. Something inside of her seemed to relax.

She walked around, touching the bed, and the lamp, remembering the clock. She could hardly believe that at one point she was ready to walk away without a second thought. How different everything seemed now!

Standing in front of the mirror she smiled at her own reflection. A healthy, trim, and happy woman with a bright future stared back at her. She'd made the right decision.

The closet was next to the mirror.

Absently, she pushed one of the louvered doors open. It stood empty, but that was what she expected. She tried the other door, and this time found a hanging clothes bag suspended from the rod.

Jennifer cocked her head.

That was strange. Had someone forgotten their luggage?

But nobody had stayed in this wing recently. Perhaps it was Malachai's. Curious, she removed the bag from the pole. It was heavier than she expected. Jennifer laid the bag lengthwise on the bed and slowly unzipped it. She opened the flap and glancing inside, took a step back.

A woman's formal evening gown lay in front of her.

She stared at it.

Had a woman stayed here?

If so, when and why?

And who was she?

A tinge of anger flared up inside her and she began rummaging through the bag's contents. Stockings, high-heeled shoes, a velvet evening bag . . . a gun.

A gun.

Her eyes fixated on it and suddenly, time itself seemed to stop. Then the room spun, confusion overwhelming her. Jennifer dropped to her knees, her breath coming in shallow, stifled bursts as memories, fragmented and jagged, slammed into her mind. The gun dropped from her hand as she collapsed, face forward onto the floor.

* * *

Shade stood in front of the bathroom mirror and tried to compose herself. She was shaking. It was still difficult to believe it was real, that she was actually here and had really lived it.

All of it.

The pieces continued to swim through her head, chaotic and incomplete. It would take time to sort it out, but what was paramount was that she not break character. Not give the slightest indication that she had remembered. To do so would jeopardize everything . . . including her life.

No, she would have to continue the masquerade a while longer. Until she could figure a way out.

114

Chapter 8

Vogel studied Shade's face like a Rorschach test, trying to determine whether she was telling the truth. There was an air of sincerity about her story that made it difficult not to trust her. Then again, sincerity could be misleading.

"Why didn't you mention any of this before?" said Vogel.

"There wasn't time," said Shade. "Besides, if I had come back without you and the disc, it would have looked suspicious. There would have been questions."

Vogel frowned. "All right," she said, hesitantly. "How do we get out of here?"

* * *

The professor looked at the computer screen a second time and rubbed his forehead. His notes were as clear as day, and he had used up every tactic he could think of to delay recreating the experiment. Now the dark-haired man suspected he was stalling.

He was correct.

Blackmarr didn't want any part of what was going on. Unfortunately, he had no choice.

"Professor?" the assistant asked a second time. "Are we ready to begin?"

Blackmarr turned from the screen. "Yes." He sighed. "We're ready to begin."

"Then, if you'll be so kind as to give the first instruction."

The man with the beard had spared no expense. The professor was sitting in a lab that made the one at the university seem trivial. It was twice as large and had been outfitted with the most modern supplies and equipment. In addition, he'd even been given a staff, ready to carry out his orders. Where did he get the money? he thought. It didn't matter. He didn't want to know.

Blackmarr took a long deep breath and removed his glasses. "Let's begin with step one."

* * *

Richard Davis sat on the edge of his small bed when the light in his cell inexplicably went out. An emergency lamp, near the ceiling, switched on, bathing the room in a red glow. A moment later, the door swung open. Davis turned to see two silhouetted figures moving toward him. He recognized Vogel's hat.

"What's going on?" he asked.

"We're escaping," said Vogel, pulling him to his feet.

"Where have you been?" said Davis. "Do you know what I've been through down here? I don't know anything. Nobody will believe me!"

"Now isn't the time," said the other silhouette. "We need to keep moving."

The two of them hustled him to the doorway, and Davis glanced at Vogel, her eyes glowing like a sorceress. "Who is that?" he asked.

"That's Shade."

"Shade?" he gasped, in disbelief.

"Yes."

"Shade's the reason we're in here!"

"Davis—"

"Vogel, are you nuts?!"

"Davis, move!" said Vogel, practically throwing him into the hall.

* * *

The two of them followed Shade, who alone knew the layout of the estate. It looked like Halloween, thought Vogel. Or at least a bad version of it. The emergency lights threw weird shadows, making it difficult to tell where to walk. Shade had tapped into the estate's computer system and convinced it that a power outage had taken place. The deception should buy them enough time to rescue the professor and get out.

Provided nothing went wrong.

A phrase Vogel hated.

"Where is he?" said Vogel as they turned a corner.

"The lab is at the other end of the compound," said Shade. "We'll have to hurry."

"Swell." She held the edge of her hat, as they dashed down the corridor. "Why haven't you tried anything like this before?"

"There's more at stake this time."

"Like what?"

"He's insane."

"I know that. He wants to take over the world. It's called megalomania."

"That's not what I mean."

Vogel glanced at her as they ran. "What are you talking about?"

"Vogel, it's unbelievable! He's going to—"

Davis interrupted. "Can this wait until we've actually gotten out of here?"

Vogel didn't answer. She had a much bigger problem to deal with. The hallway was a dead end.

* * *

Malachai had been listening to Chopin when the room went black. He fumbled in his desk for a flashlight when someone knocked on the door. "Yes?"

The door opened, revealing the outline of the butler, Arthur, eerily backlit by red, emergency lights. "Sir," he said, like a figure from a zombie movie, "there appears to be a problem."

"Thank you, Arthur, I've noticed. Now would you mind telling me WHAT the problem is?"

"I'm afraid I don't know, sir. From what we can tell, there's been an outage of some kind."

"Of course, there's been an outage!" Malachai said, flipping through another drawer. "We can all see that!" Malachai stood up straight, still not finding what he was looking for. He glanced at Arthur, who looked like a wax statue. "Arthur?"

"Yes, sir."

"DO something!"

"Of course, sir. What would you like me to do, sir?"

"Get the lights on!"

* * *

They had reached the other end of the building and were standing outside the laboratory. An expression of stunned disbelief veiled Vogel's face as Shade

119

finished talking. Davis stood to one side, looking equally shocked.

"He's going to assassinate the Nouvik of Aren?" he repeated.

Shade nodded, soberly. "Now do you understand?"

"Good God," whispered Vogel, slowly.

"Do you have any idea what that will mean?" asked Davis.

"Yes," said Vogel. "It will be a nightmare."

The implications were staggering. The Nouvik of Aren was officially appointed to the jurisdiction between Kai and West Maver within the borders of Kaskaria. However, his influence was much greater. Kings and rulers of all types had sought his wisdom, advice, and counsel since the time of King Arthur. He was a global figure whose thoughts and opinions captured headlines and who was admired by the majority of the world's leaders. His assassination would be catastrophic.

"That's exactly what he's counting on," said Shade.

"What do you mean?" said Davis.

Vogel started to speak but the gun stopped her. The cold barrel of the gun pressed against her temple. Her pulse raced as the man's voice cut through the shadows

"Don't move." She couldn't see who was behind it. "The Revolution has begun."

* * *

The man with white hair glared down the barrel at the woman. This had been predictable. He knew she would never cooperate. Anyone could see that. But it didn't matter now. The plan was in motion, and that was what was important.

"What revolution?" said the woman.

"I think you know," the man hissed. "Now, move! All of you, away from the door!"

The three of them looked at him in shock, then slowly began backing away. His gaze never left them. The other man, the reporter, hesitated at first, then took a step, tripped, and fell forward.

"Aaghh!"

The white-haired man glanced toward the direction of the sound but could see only shadows. In another moment he felt the impact of a a fist slamming into his skull. Stars flew through his field of vision, and his knees went weak. As he went down, his last thought was that it had been predictable.

* * *

Richard Davis staggered to his feet, breathing hard. His hands shook, but the gunman was down—and for the moment, they were still alive."

Vogel looked at him. "Was that planned?" she said.

"Sort of. Anyway, it worked."

Shade nodded. "Nicely done."

"Thanks. Now can we please get the hell out of here?"

Chapter 9

"I think we should split up," said Vogel, looking at Shade. The glow from the emergency lights on the wall giving her an unearthly appearance.

"Split up?!" said Davis. "Are you crazy?!"

"Agreed." Shade nodded to Vogel. "I can get him and the professor out."

"And I'll look for Malachai," said Vogel. "We'll meet at the safe house. If anything happens, make sure you tell Twelve everything."

"Understood."

"Hold it," Davis interjected. "You're leaving . . . to chase after THAT guy?"

"Richard, not now," Vogel breathed coolly.

"These people are dangerous, Lora," said Davis. "And in case you've forgotten, you don't have a gun."

Vogel looked at Shade, whose eyes had grown wider. "He does have a point."

Shade reached a hand under her coat to the small of her back. When it returned, a gun lay in her palm. "You can take mine."

Vogel shook her head. "I'll take his." She kneeled next to the unconscious man on the floor and pried his pistol loose.

Davis grimaced. "I don't like this."

"I'll be fine." The weight of the metal felt strong and reassuring in her hand, and she checked to ensure the weapon was loaded. "Keep them safe."

Shade nodded. "Be careful."

* * *

Malachai took a flashlight from the bottom drawer of his other filing cabinet. What it was doing there was up for speculation. The important thing was it was there. He pushed the plastic button on the side and a welcome beam of light exploded into the room. Waving it across the walls of his study, he found the doorway and started for it. There was a breaker panel somewhere in this part of the building and he was going to find it.

Stepping into the hall, he pointed the circle of light ahead of him on the carpet. He hated interruptions during his meditation period, and that was what all this was.

An interruption.

Someone had turned on a coffeemaker and a microwave oven at the same time and tripped a breaker. State-of-the-art technology had its benefits, but there were also headaches. He often felt there was a great deal to be said for a simple guard tower over an elaborate security system.

Turning a corner, he passed a small table and a planter. On top of everything else, he had been listening to Chopin! One of his favorite composers. Classical music always helped him think, and right now there was a great deal to think about. He had been reviewing the Vogel issue again, and in studying her dossier had stumbled on something he hadn't noticed before. Perhaps it wasn't necessary to eliminate her after all. There might be a more reasonable, more humane solution. Malachai despised unnecessary violence and someone of Vogel's intelligence, skill, and ability would undoubtedly be an asset to the organization. Perhaps he could simply—

He felt the cold steel of the gun touch the back of his head. Malachai halted in mid-step and instantly froze. There was no need to ask who was holding it.

* * *

Shade watched Vogel disappear into the shadows, as the man on the floor began making a gurgling sound. She looked at Richard Davis, who was shaking, his eyes bulging out of their sockets. He was obviously terrified. She took stock of him. He had no training, and he was male. Which meant he didn't have a deep center of calm to draw from. That was going to be a problem. But she would handle it.

"Come on," she said evenly. "This way."

The body on the floor began to move and Shade grabbed Davis's hand, pulling him.

"This way!"

* * *

Vogel cocked her head and stared at Malachai's hairline. She was behind him in the hallway, with the nose of her gun pressed against the back of his skull, just above his ears. She licked the corner of her mouth and debated. Her first impulse was simply to fire. Rid the world of one more diseased lunatic. But Twelve had a policy about that sort of thing. There would be a committee with a lot of questions to answer. Besides, from what he indicated, there were others. Possibly a whole network. He could provide names, locations, plans, and timetables if properly motivated. She would provide him with that motivation.

"Vogel, isn't it?" the man finally said, trying to sound reasonable.

She hated that. "Correct."

"Would it be possible for me to turn around?"

"No." Her calves hurt. She needed better shoes.

"This is going to make communicating a bit awkward."

With keen precision, she traced the gun around the perimeter of his head as she strode around him until they were face to face. The barrel above his nose, red emergency light illuminating one side of his face. "Now," said Vogel, her eyes narrowing, "What did you want to talk about?"

* * *

The lab was at the end of the hallway. Shade ran toward it dragging Davis behind her like an anchor. A sense of panic was slowly building inside her. They were running out of time, and she couldn't help feeling that the wheels were coming off. Kaplan, the man with the white hair, was Malachai's lieutenant. When he regained consciousness, he would throw the estate into lockdown until they were caught, and that would end any chance of her escaping. It was now or never.

They reached the door to the lab. Shade yanked the door open and drew her gun in one motion. Her eyes spotted the professor, sitting at a table to her right.

"Get down!" she shouted to him.

Two assistants stood behind a counter—one at a microscope and the other at a computer. Before they could react, Shade fired four times. The sound cut through the air like a nuclear bomb, sending smoke in all directions. Red exploded from their white lab coats as the assistants jerked and collapsed like wheat.

Davis swore in astonishment.

Shade moved past the bodies and ripped the disc from the computer. Her eyes scanned the room, taking in every detail.

"Where is it?" she yelled at the professor, who sat gaping at her.

"Where is what?" he asked.

"The sample! The specimen you had at the lecture!"

Blackmarr looked confused. "I have no idea. That terrible man with the beard took it with him when they imprisoned me in this place. He said it was needed for testing."

"But they finished that already!" Shade said, a thought suddenly occurring to her. "You mean it was never returned?"

The professor shook his head. "No."

"Then what have you been working on?"

"Primarily, recreating the conditions of the original experiment. In order to determine how the transmutation occurred, it's necessary to ensure they're absolutely—"

"Oh, hell!" she said pounding the countertop with her fist. It was already too late. In exasperation, she fired her gun into the computer's hard drive. The tower reeled and fell over, spitting sparks and smoke.

Her ears ringing, she turned her attention to the professor, who had bolted from his chair. Shade leaped over the counter and grabbed him by the arm. "We're leaving," she said.

"Who are you?"

She ignored the question and turned to Richard Davis, who stood rooted to the floor like a tree.

"Davis!" she shouted. "Stop staring and check the hallway!"

Startled, Davis nodded and did as he was told, putting his head outside the room. "It's clear," he said, stepping back inside.

Shade turned to Blackmarr, who looked dazed. She grabbed him by the shoulders and shook him. "Professor," she said, shoving his briefcase into his hands. "MOVE!"

"Y-yes, of course."

"Everybody outside!" she announced to the two men, who bolted into the hallway.

As they did so, she grabbed a bottle of alcohol, a box of matches, and a sterile cotton pad from under the counter. Standing in the center of the room, she poured the alcohol into a pool on the carpet. Striking a match, Shade lit the cotton pad, and taking a step back, tossed it at the dark stain. A blaze instantly shot toward the ceiling. She stared at it for a moment, the air thick with the smell of burning chemicals, then threw the disc into the flames and ran from the room.

* * *

Malachai stared at the woman pointing the gun at his forehead and tried not to panic. If she had wanted to kill him, he would be dead by now.

"I don't suppose," he began, "I don't suppose we could have a dialogue about this?"

"We've had enough dialogue already," said Vogel.

"I see." Sweat was slipping down his back, and there was a nervous flutter in his stomach. "I would just like to say that I hold you in the highest professional esteem."

"Noted. Now get your hands up."

Malachai dropped the flashlight and put up his hands.

"Turn around."

He turned and jerked as the gun was jammed into his kidney. "What exactly are we doing here?"

"We're going to walk to the nearest exit, Malachai. And remember, I've got this thing, so don't try anything cute."

"It's at the forefront of my mind."

Vogel shoved him. "Good. Now, move!"

Malachai started back down the hallway. The red lights seemed to give the world a demonic look. He could almost believe Vogel was a figure from the netherworld, sent to torment him.

"You won't succeed," Malachai's voice dripped with certainty.

"At what?"

"At stopping our agenda. If that's what you're trying to do by apprehending me, it won't work. The plan is already in motion."

"Is that a fact?"

"Yes, it's a fact, Vogel. And one you'll see for yourself shortly. We never had any intention of relying solely on Blackmarr's competency. Now that we have what we need, our people will soon succeed at duplicating the results. So, there's very little point in continuing this exercise."

"Well, we'll see what my supervisors have to say when they get you into an interrogation room."

They were coming to a turn in the hallway when an idea began to form in his mind. There would be a momentary break in the emergency lights. A brief bit of darkness.

It might be just enough.

As they rounded the corner, Malachai pretended to stumble. Vogel jerked at the movement and as she did, he wheeled around and swatted at her wrist, knocking the gun from her hand. It vanished into the shadows. Moving with startling speed, Malachai slammed her against the wall before she could react. Her head connected with a loud thud and she crumpled, unconscious, into a dark heap. Breathing hard, he studied her for a moment and then ran.

He ran like hell.

* * *

Richard Davis was scared.

His breathing was coming in short bursts, and his heart was pounding. The three of them were running down a hallway in some part of the building, being led by Shade.

Davis didn't trust her. Not for a minute.

She frightened him. It was her fault they were in this predicament in the first place. What if this was just another setup? She could be leading them right into a trap. Davis threw on the brakes.

"Hold it!" he said, planting his feet.

The professor nearly ran him over and Shade whipped around. "What are you doing?" she demanded.

"Listen, I'm not going any farther until I know what this is all about. Who are you, anyway? Why are you mixed up with this guy and just where the hell are you taking us?" He was nervous and struggled to keep his knees from shaking.

Shade cocked her head and looked at him, then strode over to where he was standing. Putting her face within an inch of his, she spoke from the shadows.

"Richard," she said, her warm breath on his cheek, "I don't know what kind of people you're used to dealing with, but from now on, you do as I say. Understood?"

He hesitated, trying to muster up a response that would show her he wasn't afraid of her, but instead, he simply nodded.

Shade turned to the professor. "The exit is at the end of the hall. We'll make for that."

Blackmarr snorted in agreement and the three of them started again. Davis lingered behind Shade.

* * *

The exit opened into an underground garage, with vehicles of all types parked on either side.

"They keep the keys in a cabinet at the other end," said Shade, making for the far wall. "And the exit ramp leads directly onto the main road. All we have to do is—"

"Freeze!" a voice shouted, stopping them in their tracks.

To Shade, the voice seemed to come from above. A police officer stepped into view, gun aimed directly at them.

"Oh, dear," whispered the professor.

"Just keep still," murmured Shade.

"I don't think we have a choice," Davis said.

"Everyone, stay where you are!" ordered the man. "Hands in the air!" A team of officers swarmed into view, their guns drawn, and in another moment, they were surrounded.

* * *

Vogel lay on the floor against the wall. Every muscle in her body seemed to radiate a different type of pain. She simply wanted to close her eyes and stay in this position until it went away. What had she been thinking? Going after Malachai alone had been reckless. He was a lunatic connected to a powerful criminal organization. Someone like that was not going to be deterred by a single gun. She should have thought things through more carefully and not tried to grandstand it.

The floor grew uncomfortable. Vogel steeled herself, wincing as she touched the place on her head where it had slammed into the wall. There was blood. Her rear end was on fire from landing on it full force. Why didn't you ever see this kind of thing in spy movies?

The emergency lamps switched off and almost immediately the overhead lights came to life. Power had been restored. She was instantly alert. The target was still at large and, presumably, would be coming back with help. Summoning her strength, she forced herself to stand, every muscle screaming in protest

Her gun lay a few feet away on the carpet. Picking it up she tried to determine where she was in the estate. In all that had happened she'd become disoriented, and every second mattered now. A painting of an autumn countryside hung on a wall near a planter. Vogel had no idea whether she had seen it before or not.

She looked around, her eyes scanning first one way then the other, before cautiously heading east. The corridor was silent, except for the low hum of the air conditioner. Each step she took on the expensive carpet seemed to announce her presence. As she made her way along, thoughts suddenly began to crowd in from all directions. What about the professor? Had Shade been able to rescue him? What about Richard Davis? Had the three of them managed to escape, or had Malachai's people intercepted them? What if she reached the safe house and there was nobody there? What would she tell Twelve? Shade was a professional agent, but if anything happened to Richard Davis—

STOP IT!!

She didn't have the luxury of spiraling down a rabbit hole right now.

Vogel paused. The hallway now split into three directions. It was unfamiliar, but instinct suggested that the left passage led back to the main house. If she could find a window, or unattended door then potentially, she could get out. She took a breath, and gripping the cold metal of the gun, started forward.

She did not expect to meet a police officer.

Chapter 10

Sergeant Swayne had seen a lot of things during his years in law enforcement, but the cast of characters that arrived an hour or so ago were in a category by themselves. No one had brought in anything quite like this crowd since the heavy metal concert was shut down a few years ago due to a UFO sighting.

The blond woman seated across the table from him was a piece of work in her own right. Reading over her statement, he didn't know whether to laugh or cry. Taking a sip of coffee from his Styrofoam cup, he glanced at her. She was fairly attractive, but it was also clear that the lights in the guest house were not working. A cup of coffee had been placed in front of her as well, but she hadn't touched it.

"You sure you won't have some?" asked Swayne. "It's actually not too bad. Mountain grown, as a matter of fact."

"I'd prefer a cigarette," said the woman.

Swayne shrugged and offered her one from the pack in his shirt pocket. She accepted and he lit the tip for her. The woman dragged on the filter and blew smoke in a plume over her head. She seemed to relax.

"So, let's talk about this statement," the sergeant said, turning to the second page. "You have some rather colorful information here."

"Look, I've already explained this to your cohort," she said, flicking the ash. "I'm an intelligence officer working on a classified mission."

"Yes, you did make that assertion to the arresting officer. The problem we have is that you couldn't provide any identification showing you're an intelligence officer."

"My wallet was taken."

"That's unfortunate. In addition, your fingerprints aren't in any of our databases."

"They wouldn't be."

"And there's no listing for any 'see' 'fi'—"

"It's pronounced 'sigh.'"

" —agency, governmental or otherwise. You were also found inside a private home, brandishing an unlicensed firearm. The owner of said home claims you threatened him with the weapon."

"It was a life and death situation. I was trying to apprehend him. Sergeant, if you'll just contact my people—"

"We've already tried that. The phone number you provided has been disconnected."

"Then there's been a mistake. Someone must have written it down wrong."

Swayne flipped pages. "We'll come back to that. What I'd like to talk about is your assertion that 'the gentleman with the beard,' as you refer to him, is a criminal mastermind engaged in a conspiracy to take over the world, by means of an invisibility formula." He looked up at her with an open expression.

"What about it?"

"Rather imaginative, wouldn't you say? Especially, since Mr. Banks has no idea what you're talking about."

"Who is Mr. Banks?"

"That would be the man whose house you and your friends broke into."

"His name is Malachai. And I didn't break in, I was taken there forcibly. We all were."

Swayne turned to another page. "According to Mr. Banks, he was in the middle of dinner when you and your group forced your way in. You claimed to be representatives of a cult known as The Golden Hand."

"What?!"

"I have it right here. He tried to reason with you, but you kept quoting incomprehensible prophecies about a chosen one while your friends did damage to the house. Even going so far as to set fire to it. Fortunately for Mr. Banks, alarm systems were triggered and we, along with the fire department, responded." He closed the folder and turned to the woman who had grown very pale. "So . . ."

She crushed out the cigarette, attempting to buy time. When she looked at him again, there was a trace of panic in her eyes. "Look, I know how this all sounds. But sergeant, I'm telling you the truth. I mean, who would make up a story like this?"

"You'd be surprised, Miss . . ."

"Vogel."

"You'd be surprised, Miss Vogel."

The woman fidgeted in her chair. "So, you're saying I'm crazy."

"What I'm saying, is that you've been charged with breaking and entering, disturbing the peace, and attempted assault. Not to mention possession of an unlicensed weapon. Now, based on your statement, and what you've just told me, I'm going to arrange for you to speak with our Dr. Jernigan before we go any further."

* * *

Richard Davis sat on one of the hard plastic benches in a processing cell and looked straight ahead. Under the circumstances, it seemed the safest thing to do. He was uncomfortable and the flickering overhead fluorescent light was giving him a headache. But he dared not move. Or make eye contact.

The place looked and smelled like jail. Steel bars, grimy yellow walls, and a combination of stale beer, body odor, and cigarette smoke that would peel paint. It was also humid. The temperature seemed to hover around a stifling eighty degrees, and Davis detected no air movement. Several times he'd felt as if he might faint. The thought of doing so here, however, kept him awake.

The room was occupied by individuals Davis would not care to interview. One bald man in particular unnerved him. A white scar ran up his left forearm and the word "Anarchy" was tattooed across his forehead. Each time he glanced in his direction the man seemed to be staring at him from two different-colored eyes.

Davis tried again to find a comfortable position on the bench and put his hands together. He had never been arrested. Aside from paying a traffic ticket, his only contact with the police department had been getting a quote for a news story—and this was usually done over the phone.

His wallet had been taken and he didn't have a lawyer he could call. His editor hadn't been much help either. The paper was not in the habit of bailing its employees out of jail unless it had something to do with an assignment. And this didn't fall under that category.

The new position put his knees in a strain. Leaning forward he rubbed them and stared at a spot on the floor. Note to self, he thought, take no future calls from the woman Vogel.

The cell door opened suddenly, and Davis looked up. He was startled to see Vogel, being led through it. She looked haggard and had a strained expression on her face. Davis rose as the door clanged shut. Vogel stood staring into space for a moment, before finally noticing him. She walked over to the bench.

"What happened?" Davis asked.

Vogel shook her head. It's complicated."

She sat down and he joined her. "They won't tell me anything," Davis continued. "I called my editor. I didn't know who else to call. I mean, who do you call for a thing like this? What do you say?" He looked at her, waiting for a response, but there was none. "Lora?"

Vogel didn't look at him at first. When she did turn to face him there was a dazed look in her eyes and her voice was small. "Richard, I . . ."

The hair on the back of his neck went up. Something was wrong. He could feel it. "What? What is it?"

"Richard, if you can get that paper of yours to get you out of here, you should do it."

"What are you talking about?"

"I'm not going to be able to help you anymore. In fact, it would probably be a lot

142

safer if you didn't have anything further to do with me."

Her odd behavior and somber tone were beginning to worry him. "Lora, you're not making any sense."

Vogel closed her eyes and spoke slowly. "Richard, when a Psi agent goes on a Level Five assignment, they're given an eight-digit number and a codeword. It's a Mayday. A signal to be used only as a last resort. It means something has gone terribly wrong with the mission and you're in extreme danger."

"So?"

"So, I just used mine."

"And?"

"And I wasn't supposed to."

Davis frowned. "I don't follow you."

"This isn't a Level Five assignment. I wasn't issued a failsafe. The Mayday I used was from a prior mission. You're not supposed to do that. It's a serious violation."

He could hear the guilt in her voice. "So, why did you do it?"

"Because I didn't have another option. I've got to get out of here and let headquarters know what's going on."

The bald man with the tattoo appeared to be taking an interest in their conversation. Davis leaned closer to her and lowered his voice. "Look, I don't know much about espionage," he said, "but it seems to me that the whole point is to protect people and ensure the common good. That's what you're trying to do, isn't it?"

"Yes."

"Well, don't you think they're going take that into consideration?"

Before she could answer they heard shoes clicking against the linoleum. Someone was coming down the hallway, Vogel glanced toward the door to see the same officer returning.

"I hope you're right," she said.

* * *

Lyman Peters wiped the rain from his fogged glasses and studied the police station lobby with practiced indifference. His coat and hat were soaked to the skin. He'd driven through the downpour with bad wipers and forgotten his umbrella. Peters hated driving in the city, and he did not like being awakened in the middle of the night. But the phone call was not to be ignored.

He replaced his glasses just as the officer led her out. She was roughly five feet ten inches, with shoulder-length, sand-colored hair. Agent Vogel. Her appearance was just as he'd imagined.

"You'll need to sign these," the officer said, handing him a clipboard.

"Of course, of course," Peters nodded. There were always forms. He flipped through the pages, not reading any of them, and quickly scrawled beside the X. The woman Vogel merely stared at him. Handing the clipboard back, he turned to her. "I believe we should get going."

* * *

"Who are you?" she asked him as they hurried across the wet pavement. The rain was coming down even harder now.

"A delivery person of sorts," said Peters.

"What does that mean?"

He glanced at her. "I think you know very well what that means, Miss Vogel."

"A friend of mine is still in there. He's in trouble because of me."

"I'm afraid a lot of people are in trouble because of you. If you'll walk a little more quickly, please." A battered, pale green sedan was parked at the far end of the lot. It was the only space he could find.

She sped up and spoke into his ear. "Where am I being delivered to?"

"Washington, of course."

She nodded. "This is Twelve's doing, isn't it?"

"Perhaps."

"She doesn't even want to discuss it?"

"That's a point I can't comment on. Although, I can tell you that your last communique attracted a great deal of attention. And not the kind one usually hopes for."

They reached the car. Peters felt water in his shoes as he unlocked the door. Vogel looked at him with a frustrated expression. "What's going to happen now?"

"I would say that question is in the hands of the Fates. If you'll get in please."

* * *

The Kaskarian Embassy, in Washington, D.C., is the nation of Kaskaria's sovereign diplomatic mission to the United States of America. A respectable building of brownstone and glass, it is located at 6011 Benjamin Franklin Drive, Northwest, and opened shortly after the inauguration of President Carter, in 1976. The embassy represents the interests of Kaskaria and its citizens in the United States.

Gable's office sat on the first floor, past the lobby. The elaborate title on the wooden door read, Adjunct to the Faveign. Roughly translated, it meant, "Administrative Assistant to the Station Chief." In the world of espionage, the Faveign was the person to whom resident Kaskarian agents, stationed in the United States, reported. Gable was the gatekeeper and the Faveign relied on his instincts. Sitting at his desk, he tried to determine what his instincts told him about the woman seated on the other side. She had been delivered by American police, which in and of itself was unusual, but her story was something else again. Gable steepled his fingers and studied her with a blank expression.

She was thin, with chestnut-colored hair, and soft brown eyes, which seemed to draw you in. Her mouth was slightly crooked, a feature Gable personally liked about her, and when she spoke her voice had a smooth, warm tone to it that was reassuring.

Even so, there were a number of things about her that raised concern. The woman identified herself as "Agent Shade." An agent matching her description had been assigned that codename, but that person had been listed as missing in action for nearly two years. She also had no identification of any kind and had given incorrect answers to at least two security questions.

Gable was suspicious. He leaned back in the swivel chair and applied his most non-threatening smile. "Thank you," he said smoothly. "I'm very glad you're unharmed. We've been quite worried about you, as I'm sure you can understand."

"I appreciate that," said Shade. "But I do have to ask, is this going to take much longer? I have important information the Faveign needs to hear immediately."

"You're welcome to tell me any information of any kind," said Gable, "and I'll be certain to pass it along to the Faveign."

"This is dire, Adjutant. It concerns an imminent attack on the Nouvik's life."

Gable frowned, wondering exactly what kind of scenario was being played out and who was behind it. "I see. That certainly is important. Why don't you tell me about it here?"

"The Nouvik's upcoming visit." The woman seemed irritated. "They're going to attempt to assassinate him using an invisibility formula."

"A what?"

"An invisibility formula. It's completely new. Something that's just been discovered."

"Indeed? That is interesting. Shade. How old did you say you were again?"

She hesitated. "Why does that matter?"

"It doesn't. Do you remember where you were when you had your accident? The name of your contact?"

A look of annoyance came over her face and she glared at him. "I told you that before. You keep changing the subject. This is important, it concerns the life of our Nouvik!"

"I'm sorry, forgive me. Please continue. You were saying that the Nouvik is going to be invisible during his upcoming address?"

"No, that's not it at all!" Now she was shouting.

Gable leaned forward. "There's no need to get angry."

"You're not listening to me!"

"I've heard every word you've said," said Gable more sternly. "Now I'd like you to listen to me. What's your full name, rank, and identification number?"

The woman's mouth fell open. "What?"

"Yes," said Gable. "From the beginning!"

* * *

Shade seethed, infuriated. They weren't listening. All they were interested in was where she'd been since the accident and why she hadn't reported it. No matter what she told them, they wouldn't accept it. She'd need to try another tactic fast.

* * *

The woman appeared shaken. "I'm sorry." She put a hand to her forehead, composing herself. "I meant no disrespect. I'm simply concerned."

"As we all are," said Gable.

"If you don't mind, I'm very thirsty. Could I have some water before we continue?"

149

"Of course." Gable turned to the small refrigerator behind his desk and extracted a bottle. "I realize this must be very difficult," he said, turning around, "but you must understand that . . ."

She was on top of him in a second. A snarling, rabid, angry hurricane. Gable tried desperately to fight her off, but it was like fighting a hailstorm. Her face was inches from his, eyes blazing, as he squeaked for help, and then a sudden pain turned the world black when her elbow found its way to his temple

* * *

The Adjutant slumped backward in the chair, unconscious. His mouth was open, and a glazed look occupied his eyes. Shade stood up, satisfied.

Her whole forearm was numb, but it had been worth it. The guy was a twerp. A needle-nosed apple polisher, with an ego. She never liked him anyway.

Shade cocked her head and admired her work. He was out like a landed trout, but he wouldn't stay that way, and she knew she only had a few moments. Quickly, she slid the body onto the floor behind the desk and turned over the office chair.

Emptying his pockets, she found a well-furnished wallet, car keys, and spare change.

150

Fine, but it wasn't enough. She glanced around hurriedly. It had to be here. A brown sports jacket was tossed on a chair. Shade felt for the inside pocket and removed the white plastic card all agents carried. She tucked everything into her coat and quietly opened the door.

* * *

As a receptionist, Rathen's job was a pleasant one. Working at the embassy allowed her to meet interesting people and see a different part of the world. It would also look good on her resume. She had her sights set on much more, and this was simply a first step. Unfortunately, the evening shift was not very exciting.

The magazine she was reading was not all that interesting either. Rathen flipped through the pages absently and yawned. She was staring at an ad for shoes when someone suddenly rushed around the corner to the desk.

"Excuse me, I think he needs help!"

She looked up to see the brown-haired woman standing in front of her. The one that had been brought in earlier. A distraught expression on her face. "What? Who needs help?"

"The Adjunct. He fell out of his chair!"

Rathen's eyes flew open. "He what?!"

"Fell backward out of his chair."

"Oh my gosh!" she scrambled to her feet. "Is he alright?"

"I can't tell. He's on the floor and he's not moving."

She rushed around to the front of the desk, terrified. This was just a part-time job and she'd only been at it for a month. They hadn't trained her for real emergencies yet.

"Where is he?" she asked the woman.

"On the floor in his office. I think he needs a doctor."

"Oh no, oh no, oh no!" Rathen moaned to herself. "Mr. Adjunct!" she said, running down the hall.

* * *

Shade waited until the receptionist had rounded the corner before walking down the stairs. At the main entrance, she took the white card from inside her coat and swiped it through the reader. A tiny light flashed from red to green and she calmly exited the building.

Chapter 11

Gable's eyes struggled to open. There was a dull throbbing in his skull, and his vision swam. Voices circled him as he struggled to remember where he was—and why he was lying down. Gradually everything came into focus. He was on the floor of his office, looking into the face of Rathen, the embassy hostess.

"Sir are you all right?" she kept asking, shaking him by the shoulder.

"I think we may need a doctor." Gable looked over to see the Faveign staring at him with a concerned expression. "Rathen, get them on the phone, and tell them it's an emergency."

"Yes, sir," she said standing up.

"No!" Gable scrambled into a seated position—dizzy.

"Gable . . ." said the Faveign.

"Get the police," he said pushing himself upright.

They both looked at him.

"Police?" the Faveign said slowly. "What police? What for?"

"That woman. The one who was just in here."

"The one you were speaking with?" asked Rathen.

"Yes!" Gable shouted. "Exactly. Contact the authorities immediately."

Rathen started for the door, but the Faveign held up his hand. "Hold it a moment, Rathen. Gable, what are you talking about? What woman?"

"Agent Shade," Gable said, transferring himself into his office chair. "The one who's been missing."

"What about her."

"She's resurfaced. Or at least someone fitting her description has. I was debriefing her when she decided to attack me."

"That woman hit you?!" exclaimed Rathen.

Gabel shot her a glance. "She caught me unawares."

"Doesha became physically violent?" said the Faveign, his eyes narrowing.

"I'm not sure. I'm not entirely certain it was Doesha," said Gable.

The Faveign crossed his arms and stared down his nose. "Gable, Doesha Terrance has a very distinct defining characteristic. It's subtle but it's telling."

"Her mouth is crooked, I know. It's very cute and it can also be counterfeited."

"But not very easily. That's one of the reasons she's—"

"I understand!" Gable stood up again, wincing. "And maybe it was her. But something's not right. Sir, she's gone for two years with no word and now suddenly strolls in from who knows where? We're supposed to be skeptical."

"So, why didn't you call me?" the Faveign asked, sternly.

"Because I didn't want to disturb you without good reason."

"And do you have good reason now?"

Gable let it pass. "She didn't answer the security questions correctly and when I pressed her for clarification, she turned violent. If you're right, and it was Agent Shade, someone may have gotten to her."

"That's a loaded accusation, Gable."

"I realize that."

"I hope you have more to base it on than a fat lip."

"I do sir." Gable looked at the two of them soberly. "I think she's planning to assassinate the Nouvik."

* * *

A thousand yards away, the silhouette of a man's head sat motionless, framed through the telescopic sight, the rifle perfectly balanced on the compact tripod.

It was an easy shot.

The woman's heart rate slowed, and her breathing became methodical as she placed the crosshairs over the spot where a nose would appear. The black-and-white world shimmered but her focus never wavered. This was where she excelled. Alone, with a target. Cadence gently fingered the trigger, feeling nothing but cold satisfaction, then fired. Twice.

She waited for the results to be evaluated. A moment later, a man with a beard approached. He was dressed in a dark suit and seemed out of place. His mannerisms, and the way he carried himself, were too polished. Cadence removed the device containing the small cube from her arm and tucked it into the satchel around her waist. The world returned to living color.

"Excellent performance," the man said as he reached her. "Simply excellent."

"Thank you," Cadence said, coolly. She had raven hair and penetrating blue eyes.

"Again, you are to wait until you have an unobstructed view."

The woman nodded.

"Understood." That would be no problem at all, she thought. The target had been replaced and she again put her eye to the scope. In fact, it would be her pleasure. Moving the crosshairs back into position, she squeezed the trigger two more times.

* * *

Hanover stood at the edge of the clearing and waited for Malachai to return. He was

156

portly, with a ring of neatly trimmed gray hair, and wore a pinstriped gray suit. The round glasses irritated his nose, and he readjusted them as Malachai came into view.

"How do things stand?" he asked without preamble.

"Very well, I think," Malachai said, stopping next to him. "Cadence is an excellent markswoman. There shouldn't be any problems."

"There weren't supposed to be any problems to begin with," Hanover said as he started walking. "This was to be a quiet operation. A swift, necessary shift in power, done as quickly and neatly as possible, with few casualties."

"I understand," Malachai said, following.

"That's what we all agreed to and that's what we expected."

"Certainly."

"Then you start bringing people like that woman into the organization—"

"She was intended to be—"

"And asking us to alter our plans to include your wild, speculative theory—"

"It is not theory, Hanover. It's scientific fact! Look for yourself. The woman was absolutely invisible. Don't you see what that means?"

"I know very well what it means!" Hanover stopped suddenly and turned to him. "I've read all your reports and am fully versed in the science myself. I taught at the academy."

"Then you of all people should be able to see—"

"What I see is one more thing that can go wrong. Things are tenuous enough as it is. And I still say it's a mistake to deviate from our original proposal."

"The original proposal could take years, Winston. Here we're talking about a matter of months. Under the cover of complete anonymity."

"Anonymity my foot," said Hanover, walking again. "We're anything but anonymous. Thanks to you, we've involved that professor, the police department, and that government woman. What was her name? Vogel? You may as well have announced our existence on television."

Malachai set his jaw at this. "It wasn't intentional. It was a simple miscalculation of variables."

"It was careless, Malachai! Absolute carelessness! You let your pride and your affection for Shade cloud your judgment and it backfired. I told you in the beginning not to trust her."

They stopped at a tree and Malachai looked at the man. "Winston, we're going to have to expect some setbacks if we affect real change. Fortunately for us, we've been able to neutralize the situation and remain on schedule."

The glasses were bothering Hanover's nose again and he resettled them. He felt a callus forming where the nose pad sat. "What about the government woman?" he asked. "What's to prevent her from simply swooping in and disrupting the entire operation?"

Malachai shook his head. "Vogel will be too focused on her own concerns to interfere with us."

"And how can you be sure of that?"

A hawk soared in the distance.

"I've taken precautions," said Malachai.

"Precautions?"

"Necessary precautions."

They came to a small rise overlooking a clearing and Hanover folded his arms and stared into the distance. "We're taking an awful risk on you, Malachai," he said with a hint of threat. "This had better work."

* * *

Vogel sat in Banker's Bar and stared at her drink.

She was fired.

The official term they had used was "Indefinite Suspension," but it meant fired. That was how she chose to look at it anyway. The agency had stripped her of her rights and privileges, along with her credentials, and she was no longer being paid.

That was fired.

She downed some of the Scotch and water. Her second. The burning had stopped after the first and now the liquor went straight to her head. It seemed to help. The debriefing session had been a disaster. Twelve had blown through the overhead. Protocol had been violated, procedure ignored, and a laundry list of other infractions had been committed that Vogel didn't even want to think about.

The whole thing simply reinforced one of the rules she'd lived by: Don't mix business with pleasure.

She swirled the liquid in the bottom of the glass and stared at the light playing across it, creating different hues.

Richard.

All of this had come about because of Richard Davis. She never should have involved him. Hopefully, he was now tucked away in his ramshackle apartment. She would leave him there this time. It was better for both of them. He belonged with the sandwich shop chick, working at his newspaper and walking on the beach.

She belonged in the thick of things, stealing secret files and chasing international criminals. At least that's where she used to belong. What the future looked like was anybody's guess. The way things were going, she might wind up washing dishes at CJ's Steakhouse.

Vogel downed the rest of her drink. She was about to order another when she noticed someone standing next to her. A man. She hadn't heard him approach. Maybe the booze was clouding her judgment.

"I was sent in here to find someone intriguing and beautiful," the man said, dripping with over-confidence. "That wouldn't happen to be you, would it?"

Vogel seethed.

The day hadn't been bad enough already, now she had to endure being hit on by some clown in a bar. She turned and glared at the guy. He was just what she expected. From the carefully knotted tie to the tailored jacket and overly polished shoes, he was "Mr. Cool." At least in his own mind. A wolf's smile played across the five o'clock shadow, and he winked at her.

Vogel fixed him with a look that could freeze oil.

His face gradually took on the expression of a man encountering a cobra, and mumbling something incomprehensible, he cautiously withdrew. Vogel hissed in his direction and ordered a third drink.

She'd barely taken a sip when someone was at her elbow again. This time she whirled around, ready to knock him senseless. "Get lost!"

Only it wasn't the creep from before. It was Atlas.

Atlas was thin, with long dark hair, and tattoos on both arms. He was a street musician, painter, and mechanic, among other things. She hadn't sent for him for any reason she could recall.

He held up his hands in defense. "Whoa, easy. I come in peace."

Vogel saw the gesture and disarmed. "Oh," she said, self-consciously. "I thought you were somebody else."

"No," Atlas said. "I'm just me."

"What are you doing here?"

"I could ask you the same thing."

"I'm exploring new career opportunities."

"So, I hear."

She tapped a cigarette from a pack. "I guess good news travels fast."

"Not that fast. I have privileged information."

"Meaning what?" muttered Vogel, lighting the tip.

"Meaning, I've been charged with finding you. There's someone who urgently requests your presence."

Vogel blew the smoke. "Is this Mason? If it's Mason, you can tell him he's going to have to wait. I'm not in the mood."

"If it were Mason, he wouldn't have sent me. And you'd probably be carried out whether you liked it or not."

"Then who is it?"

Atlas looked at her carefully. "A friend."

* * *

Raven Park was all but deserted at eleven p.m. A few knots of teenagers and one or two couples beside the lake. Vogel followed Atlas along a winding sidewalk until they reached a set of picnic tables beneath a large oak tree.

Vogel spotted Shade sitting on one of the tables, her arms crossed over her knees. She slid down the bench as they approached and nodded to Atlas, who signaled to her in response with a wave of his hand.

"This is where I withdraw," he said, turning to Vogel.

"I think I can take it from here."

"Until next time." And with that, he flashed a grin and started back down the sidewalk. Vogel watched him for a moment, admiring his frame, then stepped toward Shade.

"You called?"

"We have a problem," said Shade.

"Several, I'd say."

Shade nodded. "I heard about what happened."

"It sounds like you didn't make out much better."

"I never even got past the front door. They wanted to label me a turncoat."

"Are you?" said Vogel, with a raised eyebrow.

163

"No more than you are." Shade walked over to her. "Vogel, he's still out there. Nothing has changed. All we did was stir up a lot of smoke."

"It's not our problem anymore. We did our part. I gave Twelve the whole story and you can be sure T.I. will wind up with the right information. You'll get your cloak and dagger back and Malachai will enjoy a nice room in a federal pen for his troubles. This isn't the first time that game has been played."

"But not before Saturday."

Vogel cocked her head. "Saturday?"

"The Nouvik is giving his annual address at Vaughn University on Saturday. Malachai knew that. All he needed was the formula."

Vogel stared at her. "What are you talking about?"

"I tried to tell you in the passageway." Shade began walking and Vogel followed. "The whole plan hinges on destabilizing the world powers. Creating chaos. Leaders and important figures will be assassinated randomly. One here, another there, and no one will be able to predict or stop it because the killers will be invisible. And the first is going to be the Nouvik this Saturday."

"But they can't. They don't have the formula. You burned everything, remember? And it will take them months to work it out again if they're even able to. By that time, Psi or your people will have them in custody."

Shade shook her head. "He does have it."

"Have what?"

"The sample he took from Blackmarr. Malachai never returned it."

Vogel froze. "I didn't know that."

"Now you see the problem."

They took several steps in silence. The moon hung over them like a beacon.

"Vogel," said Shade, "if they're able to pull this off, even if the Nouvik doesn't die—"

"I know," said Vogel nervously. "I'm trying to think. What proof do you have?"

Shade was quiet.

"What proof do you have?" she repeated.

"I don't have proof."

"What do you mean? You must have. Didn't he show you timetables? Explain things over dinner?"

"He didn't explain anything. I just picked it up over time and eavesdropped like a good spy is supposed to do."

"So, you never actually saw an itinerary?"

"No. He was never that careless."

"Then how do you know he's planning the assassination?"

Shade fell quiet again.

Vogel stopped under a streetlamp and turned to her. "Shade, I don't have time for this. We're talking about an international disaster here. Now, if you have something, I need you to tell me what it is."

Shade kicked at a seam in the sidewalk. "I listened in the bathroom."

Vogel waited.

"Through the air vent," Shade went on. "I could hear them talking in the study through the air vent. So, whenever they were in there, I listened in the bathroom."

Vogel raised her eyebrows. "Very original. Did you make notes?"

Shade gave her a blank look. "Would you have made notes?"

"Point taken. So, what did he say about the Nouvik?"

"He told Kaplan that a light will be extinguished this weekend."

"Kaplan?"

"The white-haired man Davis decked in the hallway. He's his lieutenant. Second in command."

"Got it. So, what else did he say?"

Shade shook her head. "That was it. There was some laughter, then he turned on music, and I had to get out before they suspected anything."

A light breeze blew, and an owl hooted nearby. Vogel furrowed her brow. "That's awfully thin, Shade. I could probably get us in to see Twelve, but she'll need more. You overhearing a guy in the bathroom doesn't qualify as an emergency. I mean, how do we even know he was talking about the Nouvik? He could have been quoting Shakespeare."

Shade's expression was strained. "Vogel, believe me, that's exactly what he was talking about. I know it sounds thin, but I was in that place for two years, and I know I'm right about this! You've been in the field. You know what it means to trust your instincts."

Vogel sighed and looked at her with a grimace. "You probably are. I just wish you weren't."

"I'm sorry I got you into this mess. I just didn't know where else to turn."

The two women started back up the sidewalk silently, and Vogel put her hands in her back pockets. "I probably would have done the same thing," she finally said, her eyes darkening. "The question is, what do we do now?"

Chapter 12

Richard Davis collapsed onto the unmade bed in his apartment. A small TV on the dresser hummed in the background. He lay spread-eagle, with his eyes closed, for several minutes, enjoying the silence. He didn't want to think about what happened, and he certainly didn't want to discuss it. All he wanted to do was stay here for the next month and just sleep.

Cathy had had to bail him out.

Cathy, of all people.

It was a complicated conversation. Getting a phone call from jail at 2:00 a.m. wasn't every woman's dream and trying to explain what he was doing there had taken a bit of tap-dancing. He still wasn't sure she'd bought it. People weren't usually arrested for overdue parking tickets. Even if the car was foreign.

The ride home had been icy, and he knew this was going to require major damage control. Much more than dinner and a movie. He'd need to wear socks and possibly a tie. Definitely some expensive cologne. Cathy suspected another woman, and that was perhaps the understatement of the year.

Vogel was more than a woman.

She was a force of nature, and he was lucky to have escaped alive. He wondered where she was right now. What was happening to her? Was she okay? Her face floated into view behind his eyelids.

Vogel.

She was like no other woman he'd ever known. Beautiful, exciting, dangerous, fun, and completely mysterious. Two days with her had been like a year. Would he ever see her again? Should he? They were questions he was simply too tired to answer right now.

Davis yawned and felt himself beginning to drift off. As sleep overcame him, the phone on his nightstand exploded. He tried to ignore it. It rang a second time, and the sound was like a fire engine, piercing and obnoxious. Davis stretched out a limp arm and fumbled for the receiver.

"Hello?"

Static crackled on the other end.

"Hello?" he repeated.

"Richard Davis?" The voice was male, with an accent Davis didn't recognize.

"Yes," said Davis, uneasily. "Who is this?"

More hiss.

Davis sat up now. "Hello?"

"Richard Davis . . ."

"Who is this?!"

"We're pleased to find you in."

"Hey, who the hell are you?!"

But the line had gone dead.

* * *

Mason sat at one of the corner café's outdoor tables, sipping coffee. He was scanning the business section of the newspaper, looking at the stock charts, when Vogel and Shade sat down across from him. He didn't stand up.

"Mason," Vogel said, flatly.

"Vogel," he said, still focused on the paper, "and this must be Shade. I read your dossier last evening. Very impressive."

Shade said nothing. Mason laid the paper aside and looked up at them. "So. It seems that we meet again."

* * *

The telephoto lens trained on the group sitting at the table, and the automated shutter clicked several times. The man reframed slightly, focusing on the woman with brown hair. He pressed the shutter release again. From his vantage point, he could see without being seen. An ideally situated tree also helped hide the brown car. The man looked through the viewfinder again and adjusted his earpiece. The blond woman at the table across the street began talking. He touched the "RECORD" button on the small cassette recorder and listened carefully.

* * *

"An alliance," Mason repeated, letting the word hang in the air. "You're proposing an alliance?"

"Of necessity," said Vogel. "We share a common threat."

"And the enemy of my enemy is my friend. An interesting perspective."

"The authorities won't act," said Shade. "And if he's assassinated, the fallout will be devastating."

The coffee steamed from Mason's mug. "Worldwide chaos with a single shot. It's an extremely clever plan, I'll grant you."

"It's depraved," said Vogel.

Mason furrowed his brow. "Indeed. In my private school days, I remember reading the Nouvik's writings in class. Anyone who would kill such a wise and benevolent man is beneath contempt."

"Then we're in agreement?" said Vogel.

A basket of uneaten croissants sat on the table. Mason ignored them and finished his coffee. "State your proposal."

"The information you wanted on the LMAR," said Vogel, "I'll give it to you."

"When?"

"When I'm reinstated."

Mason shook his head. "Irrelevant. That buyer has already made other arrangements. Try again."

"Your difficulties with customs can be made less difficult."

"Intriguing. But that problem too has been resolved. Anything else?"

Vogel shifted in her chair and Shade spoke, "The Triad Ruby."

"What about it?"

"We'll provide you with the location."

"Hmmm," said Mason. "Definitely impressive. But I'm afraid I lost my passion for treasure hunting. There is one piece of information, however, that I do find of particular interest."

"And that is?" asked Vogel.

"This . . . formula you spoke of. It really works?"

"It does," said Shade. "Frighteningly so."

"And you can prove this?"

"Why?" said Vogel.

"Because I would consider that a fair exchange."

Vogel fumed. "No. No deal."

"Is that final?"

"Yes. There's no way I'm turning something like that over to you. It would be like pouring gasoline on a fire."

"Then I'm afraid this meeting is at an end." Mason stood up. "It was a pleasure seeing you again."

"Wait!" Shade was on her feet. "Let's not be hasty. We're here to negotiate. Please, sit down."

Mason eyed the two of them carefully. "As you wish," he said, sitting down again. "What shall we talk about now? My favorite color?"

"That would be pink," snapped Vogel.

Shade glared at her. "Vogel, please be reasonable."

"I am being reasonable. I'm just not being stupid."

"This is not the time for grandstanding," she said with exasperation. "We're here to find a solution."

Vogel turned to her. "Shade, do you realize what you're saying?"

"I realize that if we don't do something, the Nouvik is going to die. And that lunatic will take it as confirmation to begin his whole campaign!"

"So, we should take the formula from one criminal and give it to another? That's your solution?"

"This is quite an ethical dilemma, isn't it?" said Mason, grinning.

Vogel scowled at him. "And you're enjoying every second of it."

"Not as much as you think. I can appreciate your problem. And it might interest you to know that for once, we're on the same side."

Vogel raised an eyebrow. "How's that?"

"Oh, come on, Vogel. I do have some morals. I have no desire to see such technology in the hands of a madman any more than you do."

"Then you'll change your mind?" asked Shade.

"No," said Mason. "But out of respect for my colleague, I will make one concession. Agree to surrender the formula and I give you my word that it will not be used to harm the public."

Shade looked at Vogel, whose expression was grim.

"You may not have won the battle, Vogel" Mason said to her. "But that doesn't mean you have to lose the entire war."

* * *

Richard Davis had eaten at The White Rabbit a total of two times in his life. Once, for a rehearsal dinner and again when he was interviewing the mayor. On both occasions, someone else had picked up the tab. This time the bill was on him, and he flinched each time he thought of what it was going to cost.

He sat across from Cathy Burgess in an oak booth while classical music played softly in the background. It was one of those places that featured waiters in tailcoats, white tablecloths, and several different sets of silverware. The menu had no prices and Davis was silently grateful that he had not made any major purchases on his Visa card in the past six months.

Cathy was silent. She looked fetching in her black dress and heels, and her makeup was expertly done, but she had said nothing to him since they'd been seated. Davis searched for a way to break the ice, but nothing came to mind. He knew they were both thinking the same thing, and the truth was, he didn't really have much of an explanation. At least, not one that made sense to the average person.

The waiter brought salads to the table and Cathy began attacking hers. Stabbing it with her fork. Rickard ignored his and cleared his throat.

"Cathy," he said after a few moments. "Sweetheart, we really need to talk about this."

"So, talk," said Cathy, munching a tomato.

"Well, the thing of it is, it wasn't my fault. I just got caught up in one of those situations people sometimes get themselves into, and before I knew it everything was way out of control."

Cathy continued chewing.

"You understand what I mean, don't you?"

"No."

Davis grimaced. "Okay, I was working on a story when the phone rang—"

"You already told me that part."

"Then Vogel wanted me to go to a lecture with her —"

"You told me that part, too."

"Well, you know everything else. It's like I said before, it's just one of those bizarre things that happen. I know it sounds crazy, but what else can I say?"

Davis watched as she chewed hard on a leaf of lettuce. "How about the truth?" she said swallowing.

"What?"

"The truth, Richard."

"I already said that—"

"Oh, come on!" she dropped her fork on the tablecloth. "Look, I may not be an ace reporter but I'm not an idiot. You've got to be out of your mind if you think I'm going to buy a story like that!"

Davis leaned back in his seat. "Honey, I swear—"

"This is Lancaster, Florida, Richard! What the hell is a spy going to be doing down here?"

"It was an assignment. This professor at the university discovered an invisibility formula—"

Cathy rolled her eyes. "Are you hearing yourself? Spies, invisibility formulas? You went to the woman's hotel room, for heaven's sake! Why can't you just be honest and admit that you had a fling with an ex-girlfriend? At least that would show some dignity."

Davis rubbed his temples with his forefingers. This was not going well at all.

"All right, all right fine. Then what was I doing in jail?"

"I think you got drunk," said Cathy. "She probably took you to the Rusty Nail or someplace, you got into a fight, and she ditched you. When you sobered up you were in the tank."

He had to admit, her story made more sense. He was running out of straws. Davis put his hands on the table and looked at her. "Okay, I give up. What do you want me to say here?"

Cathy paused a moment and then stood up. "Good night," she said, slipping her purse over her shoulder.

"What?! Wait a minute—"

"You're a jerk, Richard. Find somebody else to bail you out when you decide to run around with other women. I'm leaving."

"But we just ordered!" he said getting to his feet.

Cathy was already out of the booth and glanced over her shoulder. "Well, maybe you and Vogel can eat it together. That is if she's not too busy stealing microfilm." She turned and marched past several other tables who had begun watching them.

Davis started after her but was interrupted by the waiter carrying steak and lobster. "Is there a problem, sir?"

He gave him an exasperated look. "You might say so. Could you excuse me for a moment?"

"I'm afraid there's the matter of the bill, sir."

* * *

Professor Simon Blackmarr rode the elevator in silence. The man beside him was expertly dressed in a gray pinstripe suit. The professor held his battered briefcase tightly in his left hand and tried to ignore the sweat forming on his forehead. The ride seemed to take forever. Eventually, the car came to rest on the fifteenth floor.

"After you, professor," said the man in the suit.

Blackmarr composed himself, took a deep breath, and exited the elevator.

* * *

Inside the conference room, Vogel readjusted herself in the stiff chair for the fifth time. Shade sat to her left and surrounding them were members of Mason's "organization." Specialists, he called them. Some she knew, some she'd never seen before. They were all ringed around four long tables, in the shape of a square. Mason stood to one side, with a pointer, checking his watch. In another setting, he could have been a company president, addressing members of his staff. Vogel wanted a cigarette.

A moment later, the door opened, and Vogel looked up to see Professor Blackmarr enter with a thin man. She was surprised to notice that the professor was in the same clothes he'd worn at the lecture. He seemed to have aged a year.

Mason brightened and strode over to them. "Ah," he said, "at last." He grabbed the professor's hand and pumped it several times. "Thank you, Jedediah," Mason nodded to the thin man. "Professor, it's a pleasure to finally meet you."

Blackmarr looked annoyed. "I wish I could say the same. I'm not usually in the habit of—"

"Yes, yes, I understand," said Mason. "But as my associate explained, we have a bit of a problem. If you'd be so kind as to give us a slight demonstration of your discovery."

Blackmarr looked flummoxed and resettled his spectacles. "Very well," he said, setting the briefcase on one of the tables. His hands trembled slightly as he unzipped the side. Vogel leaned forward for a better view. The professor extracted a small container, similar to the one she had seen at the university.

Holding it in his left hand, he again assumed the familiar air of an instructor.

"This is a sample taken from an earlier experiment at my home. Using these same principles and refining my approach, I was able to duplicate the results in a similar experiment at the university. For our purposes, however, this specimen will suffice." Opening the container, Blackmarr set the material on the table. Vogel glanced at Mason, who watched with fixed attention.

"You'll notice the blue glow, which is the result of the freezing process. However, as the object warms, the sample gradually becomes transparent. The result of thermal dynamics on . . ."

Shade gasped as the sample suddenly winked out of sight. Vogel watched in awe again. It was still impressive.

The professor continued talking, ". . . varying properties. The result is a high-density polarized 'M field,' which captures the surrounding molecules. These molecules then become extremely compact, due to humidity and magnetic attraction. This is even more fascinating when we see that as an object comes in contact with the field, it behaves like a mirror." He placed a coffee mug where the sample had stood.

The mug vanished.

"Astonishing . . ." breathed Mason.

Vogel turned in his direction. A look of pure amazement was on his face as he slowly moved to the table. He stood in front of it, in awe.

"Absolutely astonishing."

"Yes," said the professor, absently. "I suppose to some degree, it is."

Mason stared at the spot intently, then glanced in Vogel's direction. "Vogel, could I speak with you privately?"

* * *

Mason held the door open for Vogel as they stepped into the hallway, letting it click shut behind him. "Vogel," he said, his voice low, "are you playing a game here?"

"What?"

"Look, if you're trying to prove a point, or get me to confess, then my hat's off to you. But I need to know what the score is."

"What are you talking about?"

Mason jerked a thumb toward the door. "What just happened in there? Is that guy a magician, or what?"

She looked at him, incredulous. "You think this is a con?"

"You tell me."

Vogel rolled her eyes. "You're incredible."

"Look," said Mason. "I'll admit it. I didn't believe you. But what I just saw in there defies logic. And I need to know the truth. Was it real, or not?"

"It was real, Mason. It was absolutely real."

Some of the color drained from his face. "That's what I was afraid of." He paced a few steps, rubbing his forehead. When he spoke again, his voice was more serious. "I think you need to contact Twelve."

"I can't do that."

"Tell them it's an emergency. You've finally caught me and I'm giving myself up."

"It won't make any difference."

"Tell them I'm about to shoot somebody and you're the only one I'll surrender to."

"Mason, it won't matter!"

He slammed a hand against the wall. "Damn, these people!" his voice was sharp. "This is exactly why I left."

Vogel crossed her arms. "Mason, it will never get to Twelve. And even if it did, they wouldn't look at it."

"All right, you've convinced me," he said, wincing. "I'll help you."

The statement took her by surprise, and she blinked. "You will?"

"Yes," he said, soberly.

She hadn't expected that and suddenly realized what it meant. "I'll have the professor write out the formula—"

"No, please!" He waved his hand dismissively. "In fact, burn the damn thing."

They were both quiet for a moment and Vogel shifted her weight. "Mason, I just want you to know that I wouldn't be here if it wasn't absolutely necessary."

"I know."

"But before this goes any further, I need to know something."

"What?"

She took a deep breath. "Can I trust you?"

Chapter 13

A computer monitor showed a digital representation of a sound wave. Landon adjusted his wire-rimmed glasses and tapped one of the keys on the console. A woman's voice suddenly filled the darkened edit suite.

". . . if we don't do something, the Nouvik is going to die. And that lunatic will take it as confirmation to begin his whole campaign!"

"That's her," nodded Kaplan, his white hair standing out against the blackness. He sat beside Landon as he adjusted the controls. "That's Shade."

"This was yesterday," said Landon. "Do you want to see the images?"

"Yes, please."

His fingers moved to a keyboard and a new window appeared on the screen, displaying thumbnail versions of a series of photographs. Landon selected the first. It was the image of a brown-haired woman's face.

"So, she's still at large," said Kaplan.

"Apparently."

"I would have thought the Kaskarian government would have had something to say about that."

Landon readjusted his glasses and said nothing. The white-haired man rubbed his chin. "You say there were others at this meeting?"

"Two. Vogel and someone called Mason. We're not entirely sure who that is. Intelligence believes he may have been an agent at one point."

"Show me."

A third window appeared over the second. This one showed the woman at an outdoor table seated beside a blond woman. A dark-haired man in sunglasses sat across from them. Kaplan shook his head.

"I don't know him. But that's Shade, without a doubt."

"Do you want this moved upstairs?"

"No, I'll tell him this personally."

* * *

Richard Davis turned his car onto Bankhead Highway. Next to him sat a paper bag containing a hundred and twenty-five dollars' worth of leftovers.

He was steamed.

This entire thing was Vogel's fault. He wanted to drive to Washington and dump the whole pile of steak and lobster on her

185

head. He never should have taken the blasted phone call!

Vasoline, by Stone Temple Pilots, thundered through the radio and he turned up the volume. Pounding the steering wheel Davis found he simply couldn't get into it. Too much was on his mind. What had he been thinking, anyway? Cathy would never speak to him again, and he didn't blame her. No rational woman was going to believe your ex-girlfriend was a spy and had inadvertently involved you in a clandestine intelligence operation. He might as well have said he was abducted by a UFO or kidnapped by Bigfoot.

Dean DeLeo launched into his guitar solo, and Davis slammed the gas pedal. He didn't notice the black van following two cars behind.

Lora "Vogel" Chandler.

Even thinking about her made him crazy. The two of them were like the positive sides of separate magnets. They repelled one another. The only sensible thing to do was to stop trying to get together. It was a violation of nature. Like standing in the path of a tornado. The whole thing was a question of survival, and a man had to look out for himself.

He stopped behind a truck at a red light. The van was still there.

Vogel had been right about one thing. Cathy was a sandwich shop girl. And in reality, they had all been sandwich shop girls. And that was part of the problem. Cathy was nice, pretty, and safe. At twenty-four she was barely out of college and Davis liked being around her. She was fun. But in all honesty, he couldn't talk to her about anything that mattered. At her age, she had yet to experience heartburn, didn't understand lower back pain, and had never known the joys of burnout, work-related stress, or a nervous breakdown.

She was a kid, and he wasn't anymore.

What he needed was what Todd had told him multiple times. An adult relationship, with a real woman. Someone who would challenge him and make him think. Someone he could build a life with.

Someone he could love.

He and Todd went back to Davis' sophomore days in college. For a while, they shared a bachelor pad over a dive bar. Then Wendy appeared and everything changed. Davis had been a little annoyed at first— jealous was probably the right word—when Todd began seeing her, but he also realized that his friend had met The One. That special girl who changes your life.

By spring the two of them had married and moved into one of those quiet neighborhoods near the elementary school. Every now and then they would invite Davis over for dinner. Those were always interesting evenings. He enjoyed seeing his friend and retelling their old stories, but on returning home to a dark apartment, there was always the sense that he was missing out on something. Something better. The beer tasted flat, and the rock posters and framed albums seemed a little stupid. Even if he didn't want a house in the suburbs, he knew he wanted more than this.

Maybe—maybe it was time to grow up.

Davis stopped at a red light and rested his hand on the steering wheel. Glancing in the rearview mirror he caught sight of a black van two cars behind. The same vehicle had appeared behind him several times since leaving the restaurant. An uneasy thought came to mind.

Was someone following him?

The light changed and he started forward, with one eye on the mirror. The van proceeded in the same position. Davis frowned. Maybe it was coincidence. Whoever it was just might be going in the same direction. That happened occasionally. He drove for a block then, without activating his turn signal, suddenly changed lanes. The van did not move at first. Then it slowly slipped into a spot behind him.

Now he was suspicious.

Changing lanes again, Davis increased his speed and pulled alongside a tractor-trailer. The van did not immediately appear. Then suddenly it was in the mirror. This time moving closer until he could almost see the driver.

What did this guy want?

Davis looked for an open spot, but he was blocked on either side. To his left sat the tractor-trailer, and on to his right lay a grey sedan. In front of him, sat a red pickup which seemed determined to ride the speed limit.

Thunk! The jolt slammed Davis forward, his hands gripping the wheel. The van had hit him—hard. His eyes flicked to the mirror, in time to see the headlights moving up again.

Thunk!

"Hey!!" he yelled.

The guy was insane! Davis swerved, cutting off a sedan. The horn blared behind him, but he didn't care.

Same to you, pal!

He punched the gas and the car rocketed forward, swerving in and out of traffic. A motorcycle lurched out of his way. Davis checked the driver's outside mirror and saw no sign of the black van. He relaxed and took a deep breath. Whatever that had been about was over.

In the next moment, it materialized beside him. Davis looked through the window, trying to get a glimpse of the driver, but saw only black glass. The vehicle was matching his speed exactly. He was in the far-right lane now, looking for any opportunity to turn off the highway.

An exit appeared.

Sweating, Davis made for it, not even bothering to read the name. The van charged after him in pursuit. Another turn. The van hung on. He floored the accelerator, having no idea where he was going, with the headlights looming behind him like angry eyes.

Davis yanked the wheel left, tires screeching. It was almost on top of him now. His chest tightened as the road narrowed to a dead end. No exit. No way out. He was trapped.

* * *

Shade rubbed her eyes and the back of her neck. She was tired. Everyone in the room was tired. It was visible in their expressions. They had been working the problem for hours and yet nothing had been accomplished. The small space on the table remained empty. The professor had explained that the unique properties of the "M field" even canceled out UV rays. Nothing, save freezing, seemed capable of rendering the object visible. Which meant that with less than forty-eight hours left, they were no closer to a solution than when they started.

Shade had an uneasy feeling that had been growing in her stomach. A feeling that maybe what they were trying to do was impossible.

How exactly do you catch an invisible person?

Vogel stood up and ran a hand through her hair. She turned to Shade. "I'm going for a cigarette."

"I'll go with you."

"You don't smoke."

"I need to clear my head."

* * *

Outside, the sun had dropped behind the skyline and dusk had settled. Shade and Vogel walked along a narrow sidewalk, past a row of streetlamps to a small courtyard. Vogel stopped at a bench and took a cigarette from her purse. Shade watched as she lit the end.

"You know that's bad for you, Lora," she frowned, wrinkling her nose.

"I know." Vogel blew the smoke in a plume over her head. "Richard is always telling me it's like kissing an ashtray."

Shade smiled. "Do you like kissing Richard?"

"Are we going to talk about my love life now?"

"Would you rather talk about the formula?"

"Not especially."

They sat down on the metal bench and Shade turned to her. "You like him, don't you?"

Vogel flicked her cigarette absently. "Does it show?"

"Yes."

"How does it show?"

"I'm not going to tell you."

"Wench," she said, dragging on the filter.

"Shrew."

Vogel exhaled through her nose and her expression softened. "Why do you ask?"

"Because I've never seen you like this before."

"Like what?"

"In love."

"You think I'm in love?"

"Without a doubt." Shade nodded.

Vogel laughed. "You're starting to sound like Twelve."

"Lora, you glow like a schoolgirl whenever you're around him. Even your eyes dance."

"Doesha, my eyes don't dance, and I haven't glowed since I was sixteen."

"Whatever you say. But you're still in love with him."

The cigarette was tossed to the ground and Vogel crushed it out with her heel. "Maybe I am," she mumbled.

They grew silent for a moment and Shade leaned closer. "Does he know?"

"Yes," said Vogel. "He asked me to marry him."

"Lora, that's wonderful!"

"I told him 'no.'"

"Why?"

"Because he doesn't want me."

"What are you talking about? Of course, he does!"

"No, he doesn't." She stood up and pulled another cigarette from her purse. Shade grabbed it from her hand.

"Put that away and talk to me. Now, why won't you let your boy marry you?"

"Doesha, you know what this business does to couples. I never know where I'm going to be, he never knows when he's going to see me . . ."

"That's an excuse."

"Anyway, I'm a mess. I'm moody, I can't quit smoking, I'm a lousy cook and I don't know how to use the washing machine." She took a third cigarette from her purse and this time Shade let her light it. "Richard doesn't need a woman like that," she said exhaling softly. "He needs someone like that sandwich shop girl. Some nice, pretty, unassuming little thing who will cook and clean for him and listen patiently to his stories about the newspaper and college."

Shade eyed her carefully. "Is that what he needs, or what you want him to need?"

"What do you mean by that?"

"I mean that he chose you. He didn't have to. He asked you because he wanted to."

"But he's going around with that Cathy girl."

"Because you sent him away. Lora, I've got two eyes. And his were on you the whole time you were together."

The hint of a grin played at Vogel's mouth. "Really?"

"Yes, really. Trust me. He's a good catch. What is it you're not telling me?"

She held the cigarette and looked at Shade. "I don't know if I can do it."

"Do what?"

"Any of it. Romance, relationship, the whole nine yards. Doesha, I don't know how. The last boyfriend I had was in high school."

"I think you're doing fine." She smiled. "Just listen to yourself."

Vogel started to speak when her eyes suddenly widened, and her mouth fell open in surprise.

"What?" said Shade.

"Doe, that's it!"

"What's it?"

"Listen to it!" She put a hand on her forehead. "Good grief, we've been doing it all wrong!"

* * *

Malachai stood at the window of the tastefully appointed room and looked out down on the city below. His thoughts had turned to the world as it soon would be. Clean air and water. Safe cities for families and children to walk in. Homes and food for the population, and most importantly, education and employment programs that

194

took into consideration the abilities and desires of the individual. He could see it all now! A world where government and the blind desire for power were finally harnessed. Where they could no longer—

He heard the door to the room suddenly open. Glancing over his shoulder, he saw Kaplan.

"Yes?" said Malachai.

"We have him, sir."

"Very well. Bring him in."

He nodded and a moment later, a disheveled-looking younger man was led inside.

Malachai waved a hand. "Leave us," he said to Kaplan, who silently exited and shut the door behind him. Malachai turned to the younger man. "Mr. Richard Davis of Lancaster, Florida. Top reporter for The Lancaster Chronicle, if I'm not mistaken," he said, walking over. "We meet again."

Davis stared at him. "Apparently so."

"I hope you haven't been inconvenienced."

"No, I always enjoy being forced off the road and manhandled into a van in the middle of the night. It's a regular thrill."

Malachai brushed the remark aside. "My apologies for the abruptness of our last encounter, but in all honesty, your presence has proven a bit—well, let's just say you've made the game more interesting."

"I do what I can."

"Oh, please don't misunderstand. I enjoy a challenge. Challenge is what life is all about. It's just that, until recently, we weren't sure how to adapt your presence into our plans."

"Is that a fact?"

"Yes. But as often happens, things like this result in fascinatingly unexpected solutions. And you, Mr. Davis, have provided a wonderful solution to a very perplexing problem."

"Have I?"

"Indeed."

Davis studied the room. "I don't suppose it would be possible to sit down?"

"Oh, please," Malachai smiled and indicated an armchair. "Do make yourself comfortable."

Davis sat down in the chair.

"Would you like anything?"

"A beer would be nice."

"One beer," Malachai said, opening a panel in the wall. He removed a bottle from a recessed refrigerator, then slid the panel back in place. "Do you prefer a glass?"

Davis shook his head and accepted the bottle. He took a long drink as Malachai sat down across from him.

"This is not bad," Davis said after swallowing. "Is it imported?"

"Direct from Holland."

Richard took another drink and raised an eyebrow. "I suppose I'm going to find out eventually, but just what exactly did you want to see me about?"

Malachai smiled again. "Straight to the point, eh Richard? Like any good journalist."

"You could say that." He set the bottle on an end table. "All of this has something to do with Vogel, doesn't it?"

"It does indeed. Fascinating woman, wouldn't you say? However did you meet her?"

"Let's just skip the preamble and get to whatever it is you're leading up to. What am I doing here?"

Malachai leaned forward and the smile vanished. "Very well. Young Richard Davis, you're about to play a significant part in the changing of history."

Chapter 14

"Sound?" Blackmarr repeated. They were back inside the conference room, standing near a table.

Vogel nodded. "You said this thing generates some kind of field. Why can't we home in on it somehow?"

Mason stepped closer to where she was standing. "Intriguing idea, Vogel," he said. "Quite intriguing. Professor, is there any way we could 'home in on it,' as my colleague suggests?"

Blackmarr looked thoughtful. "Well, an oscillating 'M Field' would polarize particles in the surrounding air."

"What does that mean in plain English?"

The professor shot him an annoyed glance. "As I was explaining, this disturbance of particles creates an electrical imbalance, resulting in minute discharges. These discharges would be easily detectable."

Shade furrowed her brow. "You're talking about static electricity, aren't you?"

"The electrostatic phenomenon, yes, exactly," said Blackmarr, animated.

Mason smiled. "And this static electricity would be detectable how exactly?"

"Oh, a common amplitude modulation receiver would be sensitive enough."

"AM radio?" he said, still smiling.

"But the result would merely be random noise."

Vogel suddenly looked at Mason, who seemed to already understand. "Radio static," she said, a bit surprised.

Shade's eyes widened. "Of course. We used to hear that when Dad listened to the news."

"Precisely," said Blackmarr. "Some call it 'white noise.' It's often found in between . . ."

"In between stations," Mason maneuvered. He put a hand on Blackmarr's shoulder. "Professor, can you show me what would be involved in something like this?"

Blackmarr's eyebrows went up. "Ah, now that's the interesting part. It just so happens that we're dealing with . . ."

Vogel watched as the three of them started toward a dry-erase board. She waited until the professor began writing with a colored marker, then slipped out the side door.

* * *

Inside the ladies' room, Vogel leaned against the counter and took another breath.

She exhaled slowly and gradually her vision cleared and the nausea subsided. But the pain in her stomach remained. It had been there ever since Washington, D.C. Her conscience was physically attacking her.

What about Richard Davis?

Her last memory was of abandoning him in a holding cell in Lancaster, Florida. Not her finest moment by any stretch of the imagination. Davis should have kicked her in the butt. It would have been the first intelligent thing he'd done since they'd met.

Shade was right.

She'd been in love with him since the beginning. And that scared her. Because falling in love meant you were vulnerable. The one thing Agent Vogel would never permit herself to be.

Maybe this had been a mistake.

Vogel looked in the mirror and swallowed. The woman staring back was angry, confused—miserable. So, Kristy Hubbard had never leaped from a skyscraper or stared down an international criminal with a loaded gun. She wasn't lonely. And that was Agent Vogel's dirty little secret. Her Achilles heel.

She was lonely.

Take all the exciting missions, all the fantastic locales, all the adrenaline, all the booze, all the cigarettes in the world, boil everything down and it still didn't make that hollow, empty feeling in the center of your chest go away. The one that descended on you when the lights went out.

Only Richard Davis could do that.

Only when she was with him did she feel wanted and needed. Treasured. And only when he kissed her did she feel truly happy.

Vogel sighed, exhausted. "All right," she said to her reflection. "You win. We're in love."

But would he want her back? The police station may well have been the final straw. More importantly, was he alright?

Vogel grabbed her purse and made for the door. She had to find a phone.

* * *

8:00 a.m. Crestview Beach. Lancaster, Florida. Gulls squawked and cawed at one another in a cloudless sky, as colored towels began dotting the sand. A few brave souls ventured into the surf.

The living room curtains of Richard Davis' apartment were partially open, allowing the morning sun to paint a pattern on the paneled wall. In the kitchen, unwashed plates sat in the sink and an automated coffeemaker held a half-empty carafe. At one end of the counter, a cordless phone rested in a charger beside an answering machine. On the wall beside it hung a small, cluttered bulletin board and a calendar for the previous month. A woman in a bikini looked down from the calendar as the phone began ringing. At the fourth ring, the machine engaged.

"This is Richard Davis," the prerecorded message said through a plastic speaker. "Leave your name, number, and message and I'll get back to you."

There was a beep and a small red light flickered as the machine began recording. An empty hiss rose from the speaker, but no one spoke. After several seconds the machine switched off and a green light blinked, indicating several messages were waiting.

Silence returned to the apartment, and a gull looked in through the living room curtains, as the sun continued to paint a pattern on the wall.

* * *

Mason rechecked his black bowtie as Vogel put down the desk phone. Her expression was a mixture of anguish and concern. He pretended not to notice and slipped on the white jacket. The corner office was outfitted with a mirrored wall, giving the illusion of more space.

"No answer from your boyfriend?" said Mason, not looking at her.

"No," Vogel said, not contradicting him.

Mason studied his reflection. Along with the bow tie, he was dressed in dark pants and a white shirt. The tasteful logo over the pocket read, "Baldini's Catering."

"Could be anything," he said, choosing his words. "Man's a reporter. Odd hours. Deadlines. Probably at the office working on a story."

"I tried the office last night," Vogel said, flatly. "He hasn't been there in two days."

Mason tried again. "Well, that's not necessarily a—"

"Don't try to console me. I made a stupid mistake and now he's missing. It's my fault."

Looking in the mirror he could see she was leaning on the desk with her head down. Her shoulders bent. Mason walked over, swiftly.

"No, Lora!" he said, spinning her around. "No! We don't have time for this. You don't have time for this." He grabbed her by the arms.

"Mason, he could be—"

"You don't know that. We don't know that. The man could be drunk and simply sleeping it off. He could be at a friend's house or visiting an aunt. There are a hundred different possibilities, and you don't have all the information." Mason gripped her shoulders, shaking her just slightly. "We can't afford to lose focus, Lora. Don't do this."

Vogel looked at him and it was one of the few times he'd seen her eyes wet. "I think I love him."

He relaxed his grip and smiled faintly. "So, it seems the lynx has finally been caught. And not by me."

Vogel shook her head. "Don't make fun of me, Mason. Not now."

"I'm not. I'm happy for you. But we have a job to do, and you know the rules."

She raised an eyebrow at this. "Since when did you start caring about the rules?"

Mason ignored the remark. "Look, we're talking about the assassination of someone with the stature of a Gandhi or Mother Teresa. An advisor to presidents and kings. A man with influence on the United Nations . . ."

"I know who the Novik of Aren is, Mason," snapped Vogel.

"Then you know what the result will be if we don't stop this."

"A nightmare."

"That's putting it mildly. International panic will set in, with one country accusing another until it happens again. Then a third time. And that one may be royalty or a president. Now, maybe this Malachai can't take over the world, but he can sure mess it up for the rest of us." Mason leaned closer, his expression serious. "One shot, Lora. That's all it will take. One shot from an invisible gun."

Vogel closed her eyes, and when she opened them again, they were hard.

"Let's go to work."

* * *

Vaughn University was one of the oldest in the state. Dating back to the early 1800s, it sat on a gentle hill overlooking North Glenn. With its buildings of gray, unfinished stones, gothic windows, clock tower, and arched wooden doors, it resembled nothing so much as a medieval castle.

The Nouvik of Aren had been making a semiannual address at Vaughn since the time of Grover Cleveland. It was an important affair that only select individuals were invited to attend. Elaborate passes in tasteful envelopes were sent out months in advance. A certain number of extra spaces could also be purchased for an undisclosed amount.

A white panel truck bearing the name "Baldini's Catering" approached the rear gate and stopped at the guard house. The man inside the house checked a clipboard and, after a moment, raised the gate. The truck proceeded.

* * *

Dick Wallace looked at the order form a third time and shook his head. "I don't understand it," he said. "Myers signed it. I just don't see why he didn't tell me about it?"

The man in the white coat and black bow tie shook his head. "Hey, you know how supervisors are. They expect everyone to read their mind. Where do you want us to set up?"

Wallace shrugged. "I guess in the main dining room with everything else. I'm just wondering if I ought to call first?"

Some of the people from the panel truck were already starting to unload trays of food. The man turned to Wallace and said, "Look, pal, we've got a schedule to keep. Now, you and I both know the only thing that's going to happen is that guy's going to say you're holding up the operation. You don't need the headache today."

Wallace frowned. He was right. His people were going to have their hands full making sure everything was in order. If there were too many sandwiches, there were too many sandwiches. Myers could deal with it. Wallace took the order and added it to his clipboard. "All right. Down the hall to the left. You'll see white tablecloths."

"Thanks. We'll hurry up and get out of your hair," said the man, waving at the workers in white coats. "Come on people, let's speed it up."

They started down the hall as the battered phone next to the bay door began ringing.

Wallace grabbed the receiver. "Wallace here."

* * *

Cadence walked from the building onto the breezeway with little effort. She'd gotten used to seeing in black-and-white by now and the security officer standing guard posed no real threat. There was enough space on either side for her to step around him, which she did easily. The campus had an old-world feel to it, and the covered bridge on which she walked was lined with gothic arches, giving her numerous places to position herself.

She stopped at one of the arches and looked down. Below lay a courtyard with a manicured lawn in the center, bordered on three sides by buildings. Underneath, massive wooden doors led into the campus. To her right, in the distance, sat the clock tower, its golden bell gleaming in the sun.

Crouching down, she worked quickly but efficiently. Taking a small, extendable tripod from her pack, Cadence opened it onto the concrete and set the rifle on the stand. Peering through the scope, she carefully adjusted the parallax . The stage at the far end of the courtyard suddenly came into sharp focus.

Yes, this would do.

Now, it was simply a matter of waiting.

* * *

Inside the ladies' restroom, Vogel slipped off her white coat and folded it in half. Underneath she wore a charcoal gray blazer. Stepping carefully onto the toilet seat, she reached up and slid one of the white ceiling tiles over, revealing a square hole. Vogel tossed the coat into the hole and moved the tile back in place. Glancing over the stall, she saw Shade doing the same thing. The two of them stared at each other before Shade's head disappeared behind the partition.

Vogel stepped down and undid the purse she had tied around her waist. A black bag just big enough to contain a few essentials. She hung the purse on a steel hook attached to the back of the door and removed a small, black, plastic device and an earpiece.

They had gone over everything again that morning. The device had been fitted with a receiver and antenna capable of picking up the "static" generated by the "M field." The noise would grow louder the closer you got. In theory, it should work. The trick would be to locate the field without attracting any attention. Particularly, the shooter's.

Vogel fitted the earpiece into her left ear and plugged the tiny jack into the side of the device. She slipped the whole thing smoothly into the inside pocket of her blazer.

So far so good.

A name tag pinned to her lapel identified her as Dr. Eve Allen. The idea was to blend in. With so many new faces, they hoped three more wouldn't be noticed.

Mason had issued each of them a cellular phone. Vogel took hers from the purse and powered it up, watching as the small screen turned from black to gray. She tucked the phone back inside the bag, and slipping the purse over her shoulder, stepped out of the stall.

Shade was already at the mirror checking her appearance. Dressed in a dark blue suit, with a light gray top, her name tag read "Dr. Stephanie Brown." She was applying lipstick and glanced over as Vogel stood next to her.

"Are you nervous?" Shade murmured.

"No. Yes. Maybe."

She smoothed the front of her jacket. The receiver was not at all noticeable, and her hair almost entirely hid the earpiece. Beneath the blazer, she wore cream-colored blouse and black slacks. Vogel nodded at her reflection and felt for the gun, holstered under her left arm.

Shade finished with the lipstick and turned to her. "Lora, I'm really sorry about this. I didn't mean for—"

The door opened before she could finish and a woman in her mid-fifties entered. She was slightly overweight and wore thick-rimmed glasses.

"Good afternoon," she offered them both.

Shade nodded. "Good afternoon."

"Good afternoon," said Vogel.

The woman moved next to them and began adjusting her hair. Vogel looked at Shade, whose expression was pained, and the two of them started for the door.

It would have to wait.

* * *

Mason was in the courtyard. Other people had already begun gathering in knots along the manicured grass. He pretended to study the itinerary, printed on the thick, cream-colored paper, the weight and texture feeling smooth and heavy in his hand. In reality, he was listening to his earpiece and wondering, "If it were me, where would I position myself?"

He was to cover the western perimeter, while Shade covered the east. Vogel would take the south, which included the elevated footbridge behind him. It connected two of the university's main buildings and had arcs evenly spaced all along it. Any one of them would be an ideal spot for a shooter.

It was also closed.

Security had stopped Mason as he'd tried to cross it. Apparently, the electronic doors that led to the bridge weren't operating properly. Two students had gotten trapped on it earlier that morning. No one was allowed through until further notice.

Smart move.

Unfortunately, this complicated the plan, as there was no way to know who might already be there. They would have to play things on the fly and that was always risky. He needed to get word to the others as soon as possible.

As he reached for his cell phone, he noticed a large man with a beard approaching him. The man grinned widely.

"Why my dear sir, how good it is to see you! I had no idea you would be here," said the bearded man.

Mason smiled suspiciously. "Yes, how are you?"

The man grabbed his hand and began shaking it. "I must apologize. I really should have called before now, but I've been so busy with one thing and another. You understand, I'm sure."

"Of course, of course." Mason nodded, trying desperately to place the face. "We all have so much to do these days."

"Indeed." The man held tightly to his hand and leaned in. His expression became more serious. "Let's keep things on a pleasant note, shall we? That way, the woman Vogel can remain alive."

* * *

The Nouvik of Aren sat in a private study of the Administration building, reviewing his remarks. They were handwritten on lined paper. Just as he always did. A computer would have saved time, but he enjoyed this method. It seemed more personable, somehow. His address was not for another hour, but he wanted time to sit with it. To make sure each word was appropriate, and each line said exactly what he intended. There was so much unrest in the world and so many were looking for answers. He wanted his to be words of hope. Healing words that offered encouragement and provided peace.

"Your grace?"

The Nouvik looked up to see his assistant, Andrew, standing in the doorway, holding a tray. On it sat a small teapot, a cup, and some pastries.

He laid the pages aside. "Yes?"

"They sent some tea, sir. Would you prefer it here or in the outer room?"

"In here. I can use the distraction."

"Very good."

Andrew carried the tray into the room and set it on an end table. The Nouvik watched him absently as he poured the tea into a China cup.

So many people, he thought, so many lives.

It always amazed him to look out and see a multitude of faces staring at him in expectation, as though he possessed magic words that could make sense of it all. They seemed to come from everywhere. But why to him? Why the Nouvik? He still didn't understand it. He only hoped that something he said today would be worthwhile and that they would feel comforted.

"Here you are, sir." The china cup was handed to him on a saucer.

"Thank you," said the Nouvik, eyeing the pastries. "And perhaps one of those?"

* * *

Vogel noticed the security guard well before he spotted her. He was a large man, squarely positioned in front of the doorway leading to the bridge.

Terrific, thought Vogel. This was not going to be so easy. She continued walking and the man finally noticed her and bounded into action.

"Can I help you?" he asked.

Vogel stopped and calmly sized him up before speaking. Why did they always say that? Was there really some secret answer that would actually get you past a security guard? Agents didn't ask pointless questions. That was one of the main differences.

"Yes," she said, smoothly. "I was hoping to get a good spot to hear the Nouvik before the others arrived. Is anything wrong?"

The man nodded. "I'm afraid the bridge is closed until further notice. The automatic doors are malfunctioning. Two students were trapped out there this morning. We can't risk allowing anyone else on it."

Vogel smiled politely. Just the way your boss told you to say it. "I see. Is there anything wrong with the stairs?"

"No, ma'am. The stairs are entirely functional."

I certainly hope so.

"Thank you."

She turned and started back down the hall, irritated. Now she would have to come up with something else while the clock was ticking. She really didn't like being put in this kind of situation, but it couldn't be helped. This was the mission.

Vogel turned a corner and took her mobile phone from her purse. She dialed Mason and pretended to look at the itinerary. It rang twice.

"Yes?" Mason said on the other end.

214

"The bridge is closed," Vogel said. "Something about automatic doors. I'll have to take the stairs."

"Yes, I found that out myself."

"This could make things a bit awkward," Vogel said. She noticed other people in the hall and lowered her voice.

"Rather," said Mason.

Vogel paused. Something was off. There was an odd tone to his voice that didn't sound natural. She'd learned to trust her instincts in cases like this, and right now they told her there was a problem. She tried a different tactic. "Have you heard from our friend yet?"

"No, I'm afraid I haven't," he said. There was silence. "But there is someone here who would like to speak with you."

"With me?"

"Yes, he's standing right here. Says you're old friends."

She was confused. What was he talking about? "Who is it?"

"I think he wants to tell you that himself."

Vogel heard rustling through the earpiece and then another male voice spoke.

"Good afternoon, Miss Vogel. We meet again."

* * *

Shade stepped onto the lawn and discreetly tried repositioning the earpiece. The shrill sound of interference returned. She took it out, before anyone noticed, and slipped the entire unit inside her purse. Something was wrong. She would need to let Mason and Vogel know her equipment was malfunctioning. There might still be time to correct it.

She extended the antenna of the mobile phone and noticed the red indicator light in the corner of the screen. The battery was low.

"Swell," Shade muttered to herself. Maybe she could still call Mason. She tried pressing the green "CALL" button, only to see the gray screen turn black.

The phone was dead.

Shade closed the unit and tucked it into her jacket pocket, irritated. The lawn had begun filling up and she searched the area for Mason's face but didn't see it. Not that it would matter. Under no circumstances were they to acknowledge each other.

But still . . .

An uncomfortable shiver went down her back as the reality of the situation began to set in. She was in a potentially hostile environment and her equipment wasn't working. There was no apparent way to locate the enemy and her only defense was a gun and her instincts. She was going in blind.

Focus, Doesha.

This wasn't the first time she'd found herself in such a position. Besides, she wasn't alone. Vogel and Mason were also here, and they were experts. The important thing was to stay alert and to adapt. Observe. Know your surroundings and wait for a solution to present itself. It always did.

* * *

Malachai held the phone to his ear and glanced at Mason, who looked pale. There was no need for that. All of this could be worked out with the utmost decorum.

"It is nice to hear your voice again," Malachai said into the mouthpiece.

"I wish I could say the same," said Vogel.

Malachai raised an eyebrow. "Shall we move on to more important matters?"

"What do you want?"

"The same as you, I imagine. An end to violence. Peace in our time and so forth."

"Then stand down and surrender to Mason."

"I'm afraid I can't do that. And Mr. Mason has already agreed not to interfere with our operative, lest I hand him over to security as an instigator. You'll do the same."

There was a pause.

"Suppose I don't comply?" she asked. "I'm a long way from there. Maybe I'll just shoot you and your operative instead, and end this."

"That would be unwise and highly improbable, as we both know. Besides, you'd never learn the location of one Richard Davis."

Another pause.

"What do you mean by that?"

"Ah, yes. A point I failed to mention. Mr. Davis has been good enough to cooperate with us. Creating a kind of . . . insurance that things will proceed as scheduled."

"What kind of insurance?"

"It's really very simple," said Malachai. "You can attempt to interfere with our plan, or you can rescue the man you have feelings for."

More silence.

"Why does Richard need rescuing, Malachai?"

"Because, if he isn't rescued before the Nouvik concludes his remarks the consequences will be grave."

"Grave?"

"You will never see him again." Malachai heard a noise on the other end that sounded like a gasp, and Mason glowered at him. "It truly disturbs me," he continued, "that you've forced affairs to descend to this level."

"This is a bluff," said Vogel. Her voice cracked. "You're trying to distract me. It won't work."

"Perhaps. Perhaps all of this is an elaborate ruse. There is always that possibility. But you can't be sure, can you? Doubt is already creeping into your mind. And you'll have to live with that doubt, along with the knowledge that you could have acted. Because, Miss Vogel, this is your only chance to learn his whereabouts. When this call ends, any hope of finding him will evaporate."

Malachai smiled as he waited for an answer.

Chapter 15

Vogel gripped the mobile phone with her left hand. Her jaw was set, and she winced. "Where is Richard Davis?" she said in a strained voice.

Indistinct crackling came from the other end.

"Richard Davis is being held in a small storeroom, behind the clock, in the clock tower," said Malachai, evenly.

"Why should I believe you?"

"My dear, we've already had this discussion. Whether you believe me or not is entirely up to you. However, I can promise you this. If you choose not to act, you will never see him again."

The call was terminated.

Vogel pulled the phone away from her face and stared at the small screen as it faded to black. Her legs buckled, and she pressed a hand to the wall to steady herself. Each breath was a shallow gasp.

She had to think. And fast.

There had been times when she had been backed into a corner and forced to claw her way out before, but this was different. It was personal.

You're here for the Nouvik, Vogel. That's what this is all about. Saving the world from that lunatic. Do your job.

Her stomach flipped and her hands felt like ice.

By now Shade should have taken her position in the courtyard, and the Nouvik still hadn't made his appearance. Vogel thought furiously. There was still a chance that Malachai was bluffing. That this was simply a tactic to sideline her. She would reach the room, only to find it empty. Or find one of his goons waiting for her. In that case, they'd have no idea what they were in for. Still, this was her first experience dealing with Malachai and he could be capable of anything. What if it wasn't a bluff? What if he meant every word?

Vogel took a deep breath. It would be cutting it close, but maybe she could reach the clock tower and still make it back in time to help Shade. She'd have to try.

Tucking the phone back into her purse she straightened her shoulders and started down the hallway.

It was Richard Davis, after all.

* * *

Officer Robbins looked out over the courtyard and scanned the lawn one more time. From his vantage point, nothing seemed out of the ordinary. But then again, it was still early. The Nouvik wouldn't be onstage for another twenty minutes or so. All of this was routine. He'd been on details like this before and they all played pretty much the same. An argument or two might break out over a seating assignment, and occasionally, someone started a fight, but for the most part, in a setting like this, people behaved themselves. His role was largely to remind everybody that the police WERE watching.

And would step in if necessary.

The only unusual thing about this assignment had occurred that morning. Headquarters had received an anonymous phone call claiming an attempt would be made on the Nouvik's life.

That had gotten the department's attention.

They had been unable to trace the call, but the source claimed the attempt would be made by a woman. The same woman, in fact, who had escaped from the Kaskarian Embassy several days ago. The caller was male and claimed to have definitive proof that she was a foreign intelligence agent, suspected of turning traitor. The woman was reportedly dangerous and operating under the delusion that the Nouvik was a malevolent figure who posed a threat to society.

It was an interesting story, and as anyone in law enforcement knew, you couldn't discount anything. But you also learned to be skeptical. Nine times out of ten, these calls went nowhere. Still—you never knew.

What had made Robbins suspicious was the fact that the caller provided a detailed description of the woman. Average height, brown eyes, chestnut-colored hair, and a particularly telling feature. Her mouth was said to be "slightly crooked." It "drooped," according to the caller, "on the left side, in a very attractive fashion."

Robbins shook his head. Whatever. The department got its fair share of weirdo-callers. Chances were good that this would turn out to be just another one of those. Even so, he would keep his eyes out. If the woman did exist, she wasn't getting past him today.

* * *

The Vaughn University clock tower looked like a hybrid between a modern art disaster and something from the feudal wars. At least that was Vogel's impression as she stared up at it. A tall rectangle of unfinished gray stones, with a harsh square clock face, framed by black iron, its top was finished off by a bell guarded by gargoyles.

All things considered; it was about the most unfriendly thing she'd ever come across. Getting in it wouldn't be easy, either.

Fortunately for her, security would be concentrated on the front of the campus, around the courtyard.

Vogel studied the tower. The only access was through a wooden door and a small window, overlooking a hedge.

Vogel tried the door.

Locked solid.

She swore under her breath and flipped her purse to the other hip. Grabbing the knob in both hands, she planted one foot in the grass and threw her shoulder into the wood.

Pain shot through her arm and down her body. She yelped as her eyes watered, and for a moment everything took on a red haze. She counted to ten as her head cleared.

Holding her throbbing shoulder, she silently called the door every name she could think of. There would be a huge bruise there for the next several days, but it was the price she had to pay.

"All right, so it's the damn window," she said to no one.

Vogel slid behind the hedge and stared through the window. The latch was fastened. She was becoming irritated now. Some hair fell across her face, and she moved it.

Glancing over her shoulder, she held her purse against the pane of glass. With one swift motion, she closed her eyes and elbowed it. Hard. She felt glass crunch, then heard it shatter onto the cement floor.

Vogel removed the purse.

A ragged hole now stood in its place. She used the purse to clear away the remaining shards of glass, careful not to cut her hands, then reached in, flipped the latch, and opened the window.

Sometimes it's good to be a girl, she thought, crawling inside. Mason would have had to use his coat.

Her shoes shifted on the broken glass, crunching as she stepped down. Inside it was dark, the dank, musty smell of a basement filling her nose. Vogel lit her Zippo lighter and held the flame up, throwing a tiny shadow against the wall. There was just enough light for her to notice a switch on the far wall. She walked over and flipped it on. Two security-style lamps came to life overhead.

There wasn't much to see. A small, green, metal locker that read, "Tools" sat against one wall beside a wooden table. A beer can and a crushed package of cigarettes lay on the floor. To her right was a set of stairs that spiraled up into the tower. Presumably, all the way to the clock. Vogel craned her neck, noticing that the lights continued at intervals along the walls.

She took a deep breath and sighed. This was insane. A wicked red herring, cooked up by Malachai to lure her out of the picture. She would reach the top and find nothing but bats and a ghost. Meanwhile, the assassin would have a field day.

But it was Richard Davis.

She took out her gun and disengaged the safety. Then started up the stairs.

* * *

Mason closed the phone and slipped it back inside his coat pocket. The courtyard had nearly filled by now and he looked at the bearded man with a measure of disgust and fascination.

"You won't mind if I ask a few questions, will you?" said Mason.

The man nodded. "Ask anything you like. We still have some time and I detest awkward silences."

"So do I." Mason crossed his arms. "Just what exactly do you expect me to do here? Stand like a statue?"

"Do whatever you wish. Enjoy the fresh air and the address. There's absolutely no reason this can't be a civil matter."

"How about if I leave?"

Malachai frowned. "That would be unpleasant. And I don't think either of us would care for the outcome."

The two of them stood at the rear of the courtyard, slightly off to the right. A tree cast a wide shadow on the granite sidewalk. Mason scanned for a glimpse of Shade, but he knew it was irrelevant. The idea was not to attract attention.

226

Mason leaned closer to Malachai and whispered, "Do you really believe you're going to get away with this lunacy?"

The corners of Malachai's beard turned slightly up. "My dear Mason, belief is the key to success in any endeavor."

There was something about the way he said it, the air of overconfidence, that was unsettling. "We have another, you know," Mason continued. "Somebody else is watching."

"You mean Shade?" Malachai said, with a blank expression. "Yes, we know."

* * *

The Nouvik did not realize he had fallen asleep in the chair. He opened his eyes and saw his aide looking expectantly at him.

"Yes?"

"I'm afraid it's time, sir."

The Nouvik glanced at the digital clock near the window. "So it is," he said, starting up. "And we certainly wouldn't want to be late. Not on a day like today."

"Of course not." The young man helped him to his feet and gathered the papers from the end table. "Your notes, sir."

"Thank you." The Nouvik took the pages and looked at them as they started toward the door. "Andrew?"

"Yes?" The young man stopped.

"Andrew, you've heard this several times already. Do you think I'm saying anything worth hearing?"

"Yes, of course, sir." Andrew nodded. "I think this is one of your better ones."

The Nouvik frowned. "I don't know. There's an old saying, I think it's credited to Lincoln, which says that it's better to remain silent and be thought a fool than to speak and remove all doubt."

"I hardly think that applies to you, sir."

They started for the door again and the Nouvik shook his head. "I wonder."

* * *

Vogel reached the top step with her finger on the trigger. To her right stood the clock face, with its huge gears and mechanisms that made the hands rotate. To her left was a slim catwalk, constructed of leftover boards, that led to a doorway.

"Richard?" she called toward the doorway. Her voice echoed, then died in the expanse.

There was no response.

Vogel shuddered.

For as long as she could remember, she'd feared heights. Her training had taught her to manage it, but that didn't mean her breath still didn't come in gasps, and her heart still didn't race when confronted with something like this. Because it did. All of it.

"Steady, Lora," she said to herself. "Steady."

Holstering the gun, she took the steel guide cables in each hand and started carefully across the catwalk. With each step, she could feel that some of the boards were not secure. Everything seemed to sway, and her knees trembled. She did not look down, and instead, kept her eyes trained on the doorway.

Breathing in through her nose Vogel took a deep breath and put another foot down cautiously—then gasped as the board splintered and gave way. Her leg plunged into empty air, and she felt her body tipping toward the abyss. Panic gripped her, and she held onto the cables like a vice. Adrenaline roaring through her system.

The board clattered below, echoing in the darkness as she fought to regain her balance. Trembling, she inched around the gap, and waited for the terror to subside, before forcing herself to continue.

Reaching the other side, Vogel drew her gun once more. Still rattled, she pointed it at the open doorway and mustered her courage.

"I'm an intelligence agent," she said in her most intimidating tone, "and I'm armed. Put your weapons on the floor."

Nothing happened.

After several seconds, she stepped closer and peered inside cautiously. There was no cabal of thieves waiting for her. No gunfire. Nothing. The room was empty except for a single wooden chair.

To which Richard Davis sat, tied and gagged.

Vogel's blood ran cold, and she started towards him. "Richard!"

Davis made a muffled noise and shook his head violently in her direction. She stopped in her tracks.

He was right. This was too easy.

Taking a moment, she studied the room with a careful eye. The door, which appeared new and unusually heavy for an area like this, was being held against the wall by some unseen mechanism. She knelt down and ran her hand along the threshold. It was new. In fact, the entire frame seemed to have been recently installed. Including the shiny silver hinges.

Davis grunted and she glanced at him. His eyes bulged, and he leaned forward in the chair, as though trying to tell her something.

But what?

Come on, Vogel, Put it together! They want you up here for a reason.

She scanned everything one more time, and even then, almost missed it.

A black sensor.

It was the size of a dime and had been placed at ankle height, against the left wall.

She spotted an identical one on the opposing wall in the same position.

So that's the game, is it?

An invisible beam would be projected between them. Break the beam and the mechanism securing the door would release. Locking her and Davis inside.

Perhaps, permanently.

Vogel stood up and slid the gun back into its holster. Taking a position just inside the doorframe, she took off her purse and held it, at arm's length, by the strap. Davis watched intently, behind frightened eyes, as she carefully lowered the purse until it was in between the sensors.

There was an audible click, and the door swung into motion. Vogel dropped the bag, quickly bracing herself with both hands. The force of the impact startled her. Gritting her teeth, she pushed against the heavy door, trying to hold it open. Her shoes slid on the tile, and she winced as the rough metal edge bit into her palms.

This wasn't working.

Davis bounced nervously in his chair, and Vogel strained against the weight, looking around, desperate, for anything that could be used as a tool. A rubber door jamb lay nearly out of reach. Grabbing for it, she felt the door slip from her grasp.

As it did, her fingers seized the brown triangle and in one motion she jammed it into the frame, just as the door slammed shut. Leaving a tiny opening in between.

Davis looked relieved.

Vogel stood for a moment, wiping her forehead with the back of her hand, then walked over to the chair. She removed the gag from his mouth.

"It's a time lock," he gasped. "They wanted to trap you up here so you couldn't do anything."

"I had a feeling," said Vogel. The rope had been professionally tied. She began working on the knots.

"I never would have thought of that," Davis nodded to her purse, lying on the floor.

"That's because you don't carry a crossbody." Vogel winked. "You're more of a clutch guy."

He smiled at this. "You're good, Lora."

Vogel shrugged. "It's what I do."

"No, I'm serious. You're really good."

She stopped momentarily—and smiled. "Thanks."

Chapter 16

Cadence continued to watch the concrete square in front of the administration building. She hadn't moved in hours—a skill honed in the military. Patience was an essential part of the job. She heard the rise of applause from the crowd and shifted her focus to the stage.

Someone was approaching the podium. Looking through the scope, she saw a man with dark hair and glasses appear in the crosshairs.

She leaned back, irritated.

It was not the Nouvik. Only the university's president.

His opening remarks would take at least another twenty minutes.

Shifting her position, she rested the edge of her knee against one of the arches. She should have brought something to eat.

* * *

From her vantage point, near the edge of the crowd, Shade had a perfect view of the covered bridge. It was the ideal and most logical position. Everything in her training told her so. The crowd applauded the president's appearance. She continued to watch, looking for something, anything, that might give her a clue. When she did see it, she nearly dismissed it as sun glare.

But no . . . this was something else.

A slight curve on the inside of the eighth arch that hadn't been there a moment ago. As if a section had suddenly been removed.

It was subtle, but there it was.

The president began his remarks and Shade raised an eyebrow with a knowing smile. So, that's where you are!

* * *

"They kept asking me questions," said Davis as Vogel untied him. "Wanted me to tell them what you knew. I told them I didn't know anything, that I'm just the boyfriend. I don't think they believed me."

Without thinking, Vogel leaned in and kissed him—hard on the mouth. Davis blinked, stunned, but didn't pull away.

"What was that for?"

"For saying that," she said, touching his face. "And you're not just 'the boyfriend.'

Richard, I'm so sorry for getting you involved in all this. You have no idea—"

He shook his head and started helping with the ropes on his feet. "It's okay, Lora, really. I understand—"

"No. No, it's not okay. Richard, I love you. I know I'm no good at this kind of stuff, but I do. When you proposed, I got scared, but Shade made me realize that—"

"Shade!" Davis said, suddenly grabbing her wrists. "I nearly forgot!"

Vogel was caught off guard. Both by his outburst and how hard he squeezed her wrists. "What?"

"They know about her. I heard him in the car on the way over here. It's a trap."

"What are you talking about?"

"Lora, he wants revenge. Malachai blames her for everything. He's already called the police and told them that Shade's planning to assassinate the Nouvik. They're going to be looking for her and if they find her out there—"

"Oh, God!" she exclaimed, grabbing for her purse. "I've got to warn her. If they spot her, they'll arrest her on sight. And if they find her with a gun—"

"It will implicate her."

"To say the least." Vogel pressed the mobile phone to her ear and waited anxiously. "She's not answering," she said, after several seconds. "Why isn't she answering?"

"Maybe she can't."

235

Vogel snapped the phone shut and looked at him. "We've got to get down there. I've got to get down there. I—"

"I'm going with you."

It caught her off guard and despite the circumstances, a smile spread across her face. She started to say something but was interrupted by a loud SNAP!

They both turned at the noise.

The rubber door jamb suddenly shot from the frame and fell at her feet. Vogel's eyes widened as the heavy door slammed shut, engaging the time lock.

* * *

Shade began moving slowly through the crowd. She still had no way to communicate with Vogel or Mason, but an idea had started to form in her mind, and she'd learned to act on these things. As she reached the edge of the lawn, she took her phone from her purse and pretended to answer a call.

The president was still speaking. Shade glanced around as if looking for somewhere to talk in private.

"Yes," said Shade into the dead mouthpiece. "That will be fine. Give me just a minute and let me look into that."

She continued the imaginary conversation as she drifted toward the Walton Building, where the bridge terminated. If anyone asked, her pretense would be that she was looking for a restroom. She was fairly certain she would not be the only woman doing so that day.

* * *

Vogel rushed to the door and grabbed the handle, but she already knew it was too late. The handle was fixed to a gray box with a digital timer. A readout began displaying numbers.

"Damn!" she said, slamming a fist against the metal surface.

"It's electronic," said Davis. "There's no way to open it."

She stared at the floor, unsure of what to do. Panic swirled in her stomach, and a dozen thoughts raced through her head. This wasn't happening.

Stop it! her brain insisted. Now, think!

Forcing herself to turn around, she scanned the room for any hint of hope. Her eyes landed on a rusted metal plate, about eighteen inches square, near the bottom of the right wall.

"What is that?" she asked.

"I have no idea."

Walking over to it Vogel crouched down and began feeling for the edges.

Davis knelt beside her. "What are you doing?"

"It's what we're doing, luv," she answered, taking off a shoe. "We're going to find out what's behind this thing."

* * *

Officer Robbins knew his attention to duty would pay off. It was only a matter of time. It'd happened for his father and his uncle, and he knew it would happen for him too. The trick was not to let your guard down.

Even when it was dull.

And listening to the president of Vaughn University ramble on and on was dull. The man spoke in a wheezy monotone that could put an insomniac to sleep. His mind was already starting to drift when he noticed something out of the corner of his eye. Someone was leaving the crowd and heading for one of the buildings. That wasn't uncommon at an event like this. It was outside, it was warm, and people would need to use the restroom. But it still paid to be alert.

As the figure approached, Robbins looked closer. His eyes grew wide, and he raised his sunglasses.

It was the woman!

The one described by the anonymous caller. Right down to the outfit. It was almost spooky.

She was talking on a mobile phone and glanced around as she made her way to the Walton Building.

Robbins looked at the bridge.

It was closed, but maybe she didn't know that. What's more, maybe she didn't care. It would make an ideal spot for a shooter.

Whatever she was up to, Robbins was going to check into it. He replaced his sunglasses and started toward her. This was finally his opportunity to be the hero.

* * *

Richard Davis watched as Vogel removed the last of the screws from the metal plate and placed it on the floor. He'd observed, with fascination, as she had slipped off a shoe and taken a small tool, the size of a quarter, from the hollow of her heel. The tool had both a Phillips and flathead on opposite sides.

"Where did you get that?" he asked Vogel.

"They give them to you in spy school," she answered, winking at him.

"I could have used one of those when my dryer busted."

"You'd ruin your manicure." Vogel nodded to the plate. "C'mon, give me a hand with this thing."

Davis found the edges with his fingers and together they pried the plate from the wall. Sliding it aside, they were confronted by a rectangular hole, staring from the cinderblock wall. The hole was roughly two feet in diameter, framed with rough wood, and appeared to lead nowhere.

"I wonder what this was for," said Davis.

"Probably an air vent," Vogel said immediately poking her head through the hole. A moment later Davis heard something that sounded like, "Oh hell." When she pulled it back, there was a strained expression on her face.

"What?" said Davis.

"I think you'd better see this for yourself."

He slid over and cautiously peered through the opening. It was immediately apparent what Vogel meant. The hole opened onto an immense chasm, with nothing but air in all directions. Muted sunlight from the clock face, along with the security lamps from the stairwell, created an eerie gloom, as though he were looking into the netherworld. Davis glanced down and noticed a small iron ladder attached to the outer wall, just below him. Four steps terminated onto a large metal pipe underneath.

The pipe was reinforced by suspension cables and ran in a "Z" pattern from the south to the north wall, where it connected with other pipes.

He leaned back inside and turned to Vogel. "I think this may be a little complicated," he said.

Vogel nodded. "I think you're right."

* * *

The moment she caught sight of the police officer; Shade knew there was a problem. She pretended to still be on the phone as he approached.

"Yes, I understand that" she said into the dead mouthpiece, "but I'm sure the Nouvik's remarks will still be insightful."

"Excuse me, ma'am." The officer blocked her path.

"Yes?" Shade feigned annoyance at the interruption and glanced at him.

"May I see your admittance ticket?"

Shade looked at the man as if he were a snow pea. "I'm with the press. I don't have an admittance ticket."

"You still need an admittance ticket, even if you are with the press."

"Tell that to my bureau chief."

"Can I see your press credentials, then?"

"What for?"

"You match the description of someone who's wanted for questioning."

"What kind of questioning?"

"We can talk about that downtown."

Shade shook her head. "Larry, you're not going to believe what's going on here. This clown says I'm wanted for questioning."

"Who are you speaking with?" said the officer.

"My editor."

The officer put out his hand. "May I talk with Larry?"

Shade shrugged. "Be my guest."

She threw the phone at him. Hard.

Hard enough that when it connected with his nose, it knocked him backward.

Seizing her purse, she ran for the building and burst through the glass double doors. The small crowd in the lobby stared at her like she was insane. Shade didn't care. A curving stairway sat at the far end. She raced up it, with her heart pounding. A plan was already piecing itself together. The question was—would she have enough time?

* * *

Andrew stood quietly beside the Nouvik in the elevator and watched the digital numbers change as they descended. The car suddenly stopped at floor number six and the door opened. They both looked up, but there was no one waiting to get on. The Nouvik glanced around and then, without warning, stepped off.

It took a second for Andrew to realize what had just happened.

"Your grace?" he said, nervously. The Nouvik did not respond.

The door began to close, and Andrew stopped it with his hand. "Your grace!" he repeated, bolting out of the car.

He caught sight of him. A wispy figure in a robe, halfway down the hallway, padding along the carpet.

"Your grace, where are you going?!" Andrew shouted.

"To find serenity," the figure said, turning a corner.

Andrew felt his stomach lurch as he started desperately down the corridor. "Your grace, please wait!"

* * *

Mason sat stiffly beside Malachai as the president began concluding his remarks. A man called Kaplan sat to his right. He had relieved him of his earpiece, gun, and phone. Now he stared at the stage and seemed to hang on every word the president said.

Mason set his jaw and scanned the crowd again, looking for any sign of Shade. He could only hope she was alive and continuing with the plan.

Malachai rubbed his beard and spoke to him under his breath. "What made you leave the intelligence world?"

Mason did not look in his direction. "What do you mean?"

"You obviously have an affinity for this sort of business. What made you give it up? Insufficient compensation?"

"There was a difference of opinion between me and my superiors," Mason said quietly.

"About?"

Polite applause rose as the president finally stopped speaking. Mason and Malachai both stood and joined in.

"My 401K package," said Mason.

* * *

Vogel put another foot on the pipe and halted. Her hand held tightly to one of the suspension cables. Davis was ahead of her. He had taken the rope from his bindings and tethered them together with it. Vogel looked at the rope and then at her feet. They refused to move.

"Richard," she whispered, her voice cracking.

"Yes?"

"I can't do this."

"What do you mean?"

She grimaced. "I'm . . . acrophobic."

"You're afraid of spiders?"

Vogel rolled her eyes in exasperation. "Heights, Davis! I'm afraid of heights!"

"But you—"

"I can handle it for a little while, but to get all the way over there . . . I'm going to fall. I know it." She looked at him desperately and he took a step closer to where she was.

"Lora, you've taken out international criminals in foreign cities. You've fought terrorists with a gun and a sword. You're Vogel. International woman of mystery. And Vogel isn't going to be taken down by a pipe in a clock tower." Davis put a hand on her shoulder. "Got it?"

His face was reassuring, and Vogel nodded. She winced and tried to let go of the cable, but her hand refused. "I don't think so, Davis."

He reached for her other hand. "Here, grab my belt."

Vogel did so cautiously.

"Just hang onto me and do what I do."

"Okay," she whispered.

Davis took a step and Vogel followed suit. He took another and Vogel did the same, slowly letting go of the suspension cable. Davis took a third step and Vogel held onto his belt with a death grip as she put down one foot . . . then another.

She felt the rust shift under the ball of her foot a moment before she slipped.

Chapter 17

Andrew raced down the hallway, searching in every open doorway for the Nouvik. His grace had given him the slip as they were making their way to the courtyard. Now all Andrew could think of was how he was going to explain to his superiors that he'd managed to lose one of the world's most important figures ten minutes before his annual address. It was not the type of thing that tended to boost one's career path.

He turned a corner and opened the door to a classroom. Stepping inside he spotted a robed figure looking thoughtfully out a window. Sunlight playing across his features.

Andrew glared at him in frustration. "Your grace," he said, struggling to catch his breath. "The address—"

The Nouvik put up a hand. "Andrew, do you know why the sky is blue?" he said.

"Sir?"

"It's an optical illusion created by diffused sunlight reacting to the Earth's atmosphere."

"I didn't know that sir."

"I learned it from my third-grade teacher when I was eight years old." The Nouvik smiled at the memory. "Now that is information worth knowing. It's important."

"Yes, sir."

He walked over and the older man turned to him. "This," he said, holding up his notes, "is not. What I have here has been said by dozens of other people, in any number of combinations. They're words without substance, Andrew. Empty phrases. And do you know why they're empty?"

The aide shrugged. "No."

"Because I've run out of things to say." The Nouvik turned back to the window. "I actually ran out several years ago but was afraid to mention it. Change can be very unsettling to people. I've quietly been hoping that inspiration would return and that one morning I'd wake up and get a bolt from the blue, as it were. But so far, that hasn't happened."

He stood looking at the sky and Andrew felt sympathy for the man. He moved closer and put a hand on his shoulder. "Sir, I'm sorry. I didn't know. But your address. We really must be going. They're expecting you."

"Let them wait."

"But sir—"

"Andrew," the Nouvik turned to him gruffly, then softened. "Andrew, if I'm going to have to deliver something like this, let me do it in my own way. Besides, it's not as though they can fire me." He patted him on the arm. "Come. I'm certain there's a candy machine somewhere in this building."

* * *

Officer Robbins ran toward the Walton Building, wincing. The bridge of his nose was bleeding and his face stung from where the mobile phone had whacked him. The whole thing had now become personal; he was more determined than ever to catch that woman. He pressed the button on his radio and spoke into it.

"This is Robbins. I need backup at the Walton Building. Woman matching the description of suspect, "Shade," has been sighted entering the facility. Suspect is alone, dangerous, and possibly armed."

"Roger that," a voice said from the radio. "Available backup, assist Robbins and detain subject."

Robbins heard static, followed by, "Copy that," and kept moving. He entered the lobby, searching for any trace of the woman. A handful of students stood near a wide stairway, chatting.

"Excuse me," he said, approaching them. "Did any of you see a woman with brown hair, medium height, come through here?"

Two girls and the boy stared as if he were from Mars.

The girl wearing glasses and a Soundgarden t-shirt finally spoke. "We haven't seen anyone come through here at all."

"How long have you been here?"

They looked at him again, and the boy with the nose ring answered. "Um, we just got here. We're on our way to class."

Robbins nodded, irritated. "Carry on." He started up the stairs with no idea where he was going.

* * *

Vogel hung from the pipe by her bare hands. Her feet kicking uselessly against the snapped rope as gravity yanked at her body. Threatening to pull her into the abyss. The urge to scream was overpowering, and every fear she'd ever had seemed to be playing out in living color.

"Richard!" she managed to gasp. "Help me!"

She looked up to see him holding the suspension wire with his right hand. His arm was fully extended as he bent down to reach for her with his left hand.

She stretched as far as she could, her shoulder blade on fire. But it wasn't enough. They were separated by mere inches.

"Vogel, I . . ."

"Richard!"

Panic began to rise up in her chest. Her fingers were losing their grip and she knew that in the next few seconds, she'd plummet into space.

"Richard, please!"

"Hold on!"

"I can't! I'm slipping!"

He was doing something, but she couldn't tell what. It didn't matter. Nothing mattered now. Everything was swirling in her head like a circus. She wasn't even sure where she was anymore. She clenched her eyes closed; she couldn't watch. Sweat had formed on her palms and the pipe was wet. She felt her fingers slipping . . . slipping.

Then suddenly, a hand grabbed her wrist.

* * *

Shade burst into the restroom, tossing her purse onto the counter. Her hands shook as she fumbled with the zipper.

Not in the main pocket.

Where the hell was it?!

This was not the time to dig through a handbag! Her breath quickened and she was sweating. Unzipping the front flap, she felt a wave of relief as she put her hand inside.

Shade took out the small container and stared at it a moment before opening the lid.

* * *

Professor Blackmarr sat in his study and rummaged through his briefcase one more time. It simply had to be here. There could be no other explanation.

He searched again, then hunted through the mess of papers on his desk, his jacket, and even his glasses case without success.

This was impossible!

He knew he'd repacked the specimen before being escorted from the conference room. He double-checked everything before buttoning his coat. That woman had even . . .

That woman!

What was her name?

Shade! She'd made a point of making certain he had his briefcase. She carried it for him to the elevator and even packed it in the back of the taxi.

Blackmarr seized the bag, angrily, turned it upside down, and shook it. A small piece of paper drifted from one of the compartments onto the carpet. Picking it up, he saw there was writing on one side. He adjusted his spectacles and read it.

I'm sorry, professor. I promise to return it later. -Shade

The professor slumped back into the chair; mouth open. "Egad."

* * *

Richard Davis leaned forward and reached for Vogel's other hand as she struggled beneath the large pipe. His half of the broken rope was now tied to the suspension cable with the other end knotted to his belt. He strained, feeling the weight of her body, as he held tightly to her left forearm.

"Richard, please don't let go!" she sputtered, her eyes wide with fear.

"I'm not going to drop you, Lora," he groaned.

She grabbed for his open hand, her fingers brushing his, but not connecting.

"It's not going to work," she yelled.

"It's going to work! Just try!"

A look of desperation came over her face and she lunged toward him. Davis thrust his arm forward and this time, managed to seize her palm. Stunned, their eyes connected in shocked relief.

Vogel clung to his hand and, shifting his position, he slowly pulled her up. Holding on tightly as she scrambled to regain her footing. She was panting, and her eyes were wet as she slowly stood up.

"Richard," she said, still not letting go.

"Yes?"

"Let's not do that again."

"Agreed."

* * *

"I haven't had my Milk Duds!" The Nouvik was being hustled down a stairwell by Andrew and someone named Paige, who looked to be all of about nineteen. He wasn't certain what her position was, but she had swooped into the vending machine room, just as the Nouvik had pressed B7.

"I understand, sir," Paige was saying, as she practically shoved him forward. She had one arm and Andrew had the other. "But your address. They're expecting you and really, we can't keep them waiting any longer."

Paige was smartly dressed, bossy, and perky. Qualities the Nouvik absolutely detested.

"When you think of all the important people who have been waiting for this moment," she continued, "It really would be a shame to disappoint—"

"Yes, yes, yes, of course, of course," he said as they turned a corner. "Andrew?!"

"Yes, your grace?"

"Do you have my Milk Duds?"

"They're right here, your grace."

* * *

253

Richard Davis held Vogel's hand and breathed a sigh of relief. They had made it safely across and were standing on a ledge to the left of the clock face. Immediately in front of them stood a series of arch-shaped openings. He led them to the one at the far left and peered out.

"Richard, we've got to get out of here," said Vogel. She let go of his hand and the authority had returned to her voice. "The Nouvik is going to be speaking in less than ten minutes."

"Lora, I think we're stuck," he said, scanning the immediate area. He was looking for steps, or something resembling a ladder would have been built into the structure for maintaining the clock. But there was nothing. "You haven't got a parachute stashed in your purse, have you?"

"Richard, this is serious. If I don't get out of here, your girlfriend is going to be responsible for causing an international incident."

Davis turned and looked at her. "What did you just say?"

"I said there's going to be an international incident if I don't—"

"No, before that."

"I said "—she paused at the word and looked at him deliberately—"your girlfriend."

"That's the part."

Vogel smiled self-consciously and quickly kissed him. "Okay, I get it. But we've still got to get down. And I'm not about to jump."

Davis put his head out of the opening and craned his neck. To his left, he saw a brass drainpipe. One stood at each corner of the building, running from the ground to the mouths of the gargoyles on the roof. He turned back to Vogel. "Hun, I think I've got it."

Vogel spotted the drainpipe, and her eyes immediately grew wide. "No," she said, shaking her head.

"Just hear me out. I worked for the power company when I was in college, and there's a technique to it. We'll be okay."

* * *

Robbins barged into the restroom. His head was throbbing and the pain from his nose was intense. Looking into the mirror, he could see why the kids had stared at him that way. The bridge of his nose was a bloody mess and some of it had gotten on his shirt. Robbins touched the area and winced. It might be broken. That would be his first charge against her.

Assault.

He turned on the water and wet a paper towel. He dabbed at the wound and applied as much pressure as he could stand until the bleeding stopped. The pain was agonizing. Whoever that woman was, she had issues. He would certainly see to it that she answered some questions. Starting with, what was the big idea of attacking an officer of the law? She could see the badge!

"Robbins, this is Blake. What is your location?" His police radio echoed loudly in the tile room. Robbins pressed the button on the side.

"Blake, this is Robbins. I'm currently on the third floor."

"This is Blake. I'm on the third floor. I don't see you."

Robbins tossed the paper towel away quickly and started out the door. "Copy that. I'm on the south end walking toward the elevator."

* * *

Shade didn't take another breath until the door closed behind the police officer. Her hands felt like ice. In the future, she'd pay better attention to restroom signs. She'd barely had time to slip the device into her wristband before the man had charged in.

Too stunned to move, she'd stood frozen in place the entire time. If he had taken one step to the right, he would have touched her.

She exhaled audibly and turned to the mirror, not quite believing what she was seeing. The world was black-and-white, and before her was a reflective glass. But no Shade. She truly was — invisible.

Astonishing was the only word she could think of.

The door opened again, and Shade turned to see a male student enter.

Busy place.

Stepping cautiously, she darted behind him and as the door began to close, slipped out into the hallway. A different police officer stood a few feet away, talking on a radio. She was becoming more accustomed to her black-and-white world now and silently edged by him and continued down the hall.

The bridge wouldn't be far away.

Chapter 18

Vogel was airborne.

At least that was how it felt.

Her hands were wrapped in strips of old cloth Davis had found; her purse tucked tightly under her chin. She flew down the drainpipe, the makeshift gloves scorching hot as they shielded her hands. Why hadn't she gone into something simple like politics?

The wind whipped through her hair, as she raced toward the ground, and in the next moment, she dropped and rolled expertly onto the green grass. Davis flopped down, ungracefully, beside her. Vogel jumped up, brushed herself off, and shouldered her purse.

"Come on," she said, grabbing Davis' arm. "There's no time!"

She could hear applause as they ran toward the courtyard.

* * *

The crowd rose to their feet as the Nouvik of Arden strode calmly across the stage. Applause rippled as he offered a measured smile. Andrew's notes for the address were tucked into his left hand, but the Nouvik set them aside, placing them face down on the lectern. He had decided to say something else. Andrew didn't need to know.

With hands resting firmly on on either side of the podium, the Nouvik stood patiently and waited for the noise to subside, and the people to take their seats.

"My friends," he began.

He was unaware of the telescopic sight, or the sniper.

* * *

Cadence's finger hovered over the trigger as the Nouvik's face filled the crosshairs. The waiting was over. Now it was all about timing. There would be one opportunity, maybe two if she was lucky. But you couldn't count on luck. Picking the right moment was the secret. That was what separated the amateurs from the experts. The women from the girls.

You had to sense it.

She'd hold her fire until that ticklish feeling in the bottom of her stomach. As she studied the scene, she heard the automatic door opening behind her. Glancing over she nearly dropped her rifle.

"Hello, Cadence."

* * *

A security guard stood at the west entrance to the courtyard as Vogel and Richard Davis approached.

"Terrific," murmured Vogel. "This just keeps getting better."

"I've got an idea," Davis said under his breath.

"For what?"

"Just trust me." He rushed toward the man, waving his arms wildly. "Gun! Hey! They've got a gun!"

Vogel followed and tried not to laugh.

The man sprang to life. "Can I help you?"

"Didn't you hear what he said?" shouted Vogel. "They've got a gun! We just saw him. He's heading this way!"

"What gun?" the guard said, suddenly alert. "Where did you see a gun?"

"Back there!" Davis said, pointing in the direction of the dormitories. "It was some guy with green hair!"

"He said he was going to fulfill the prophecy," Vogel added.

"Waved it right at us!" Davis said. "It looked like a cannon."

"Okay, hold it!" the guard said, looking nervous. "You said you saw someone brandishing a firearm heading in this direction?"

"For crying out loud, yes!" shouted Vogel. "What's the matter with you? He was screaming his head off about the revolution—"

"The guy's crazy!" Davis insisted. "You gotta do something!"

"All right, calm down. First, I need a description of the suspect," the security guard said.

Vogel was already pointing to her right. "Description? What description? He's right over there! Look!"

The guard turned. "Where?"

"There!" said Davis.

The left hook was well-placed and knocked the man senseless. He crumpled to the ground in a heap.

Vogel looked at the unconscious figure, then turned to Davis. "You're getting good at this."

"Thanks," he nodded, "but I think we'd better keep moving."

Vogel took the lead as they rushed through the gate.

* * *

Mason noticed the disturbance at the same time as Malachai. Shouting came from the left side of the crowd, followed by officers sprinting in that direction. Out of the corner

261

of his eye, he saw someone charge down the center aisle.

"Your eminence!" she shouted, as Richard Davis followed close behind.

Mason turned to Malachai. "Sir, I believe you're about to have your afternoon ruined."

Malachai looked astonished. "What on earth is going on?"

"Vogel is going on," said Mason. "Now, if you'll excuse me, I think I'll just give her a hand."

He stood, but Kaplan grabbed his arm. "Stay where you are."

Mason glared at him. "Now, I don't think that would be very wise, would it? With all these officers around, and everything?"

Kaplan seethed, but Mason shoved past both of them and turned his attention to the stage. "Your grace!"

* * *

The Nouvik of Aren paused his introduction and gazed out at the crowd. Something was obviously going on. A knot of confusion had formed to his right and now police officers from every side of the venue seemed to be converging on it.

What was happening out there?

As he looked on, he heard a distinct voice shouting and saw three figures running down the main aisle toward the podium. A woman and two men.

"Your eminence, please!" he heard the woman say. "You're in grave danger!"

The Nouvik was stunned. He stood frozen, unsure what to do or how to react. Danger? What was she talking about? Was this some kind of demonstration? Who was this lady?

Andrew was suddenly at his side. "Your grace, I think we should get you out of here."

Paige had reappeared as well and took his arm. "Yes, I think that's a wise idea. If you'll just follow me—"

Suddenly, the woman from the crowd leaped to the podium. "Your grace, get down!"

The words were barely out of her mouth when the crack of a rifle echoed through the courtyard.

Chapter 19

Shade gripped the barrel of the gun, her fingers aching as she forced it upward, redirecting the shot. The cold metal bit into her palm and the weight of the weapon made her muscles scream.

"I'll eliminate you for this!" Cadence snarled, stomping down hard on her boot.

Shade yelped, her grip on the gun faltering, as pain shot up her leg. With her free hand, she lashed out, in a solid punch. She saw blood spray from Cadence's mouth as her head snapped back, and in that split second Shade lunged for the gun.

She missed.

Cadence was on top of her in an instant. The force of the impact knocking the air from her body. They rolled, a tangle of limbs and rage, and Shade could feel adrenaline flooding her system. She bucked against the other woman's weight, but the assassin pinned her, a knee digging sharply into her chest.

With blurred vision, Shade looked up. Cadence's eyes were wild with unrelenting fury, blood dripping from the corners of her mouth. Again, she thrashed to break free, but the grip was like iron.

"How did you see me?" Cadence growled.

"Call it a hunch," Shade smirked.

"This changes nothing. We will still be victorious."

Shade gritted her teeth. "Go to hell."

Cadence raised the rifle high with one arm,the barrel, pointed up, glinting in the light.

"Good night, princess!"

Her eyes widened, but there was no time to react. The rifle butt dove from the blue sky like a falcon. She felt the blow and then the light went out.

* * *

The bullet smashed into the corner of the podium, missing the Nouvik by mere inches. Richard Davis looked up from the floor of the stage. Smoke drifted in near the bridge, but he saw no one.

That lunatic was really serious, he thought.

It was bedlam. Police and security guards seemed to be everywhere, trying to control the crowd, which had turned into a screaming, terrorized mob. He looked around for Vogel and saw her being detained by two officers. Getting to his feet, he started toward her when he felt a hand on his shoulder.

"Sir, would you please come with me?"

* * *

Andrew tried to keep calm as he and Paige hustled the Nouvik into the building. There was so much happening that it was difficult to think.

Who were these people, and why were they shooting at them?

"Where are we going?" The Nouvik asked for the third time. Andrew could tell he was rattled.

"Somewhere safe, your grace," Paige answered. Andrew was glad for that.

"I don't understand. What about my address?"

"Don't worry about that now," Paige continued as they rounded a corner. "There's an office on the fourth floor where you'll be quite comfortable."

"I wouldn't worry about the Nouvik's comfort. I'm sure we can accommodate that."

Andrew froze.

Two men stood in the hallway just in front of the elevators. A heavyset man in a gray suit, with a beard, and a tall thin man with a sharp chin and blue eyes. The thin man had white hair and pointed a gun in their direction.

"What the hell is this?" Andrew said, stiffening. "What are you doing?"

The heavyset man stepped forward. "Oh, come, come. You should have seen enough television by now to recognize a kidnapping."

"Kidnapping?!" said Paige, sharply. "Now wait just a minute—"

"I will not wait just a minute, young lady. I've run out of time. And I suggest that if you wish to protect the Nouvik's life you will stand there and be silent." The bearded man turned to the Nouvik. "Your grace if you will please come with us."

The Nouvik squared his shoulders. "Certainly not! Who are you people anyway?"

"We're the people holding the guns," the man said, producing a pistol of his own. "And if you don't come with us immediately, we'll be forced to shoot this young man and woman."

Paige shrieked and Andrew felt his blood run cold.

"Good heavens!" said the Nouvik.

"Indeed," said the man.

* * *

Cadence adjusted the crosshairs until they settled on Vogel's face. Below, she was gesturing wildly, arguing with the police. Cadence smiled, as her finger hovered over the trigger—just one light squeeze, that's all it would take. She could already feel the satisfaction in her body. Malachai would reward her for this.

"Drop it!"

The nose of a pistol was suddenly at her temple, freezing her in place. Her finger twitched on the trigger, but she stopped just short of firing.

"You're persistent," Cadence hissed, "I'll give you that." She chided herself for not taking the extra few moments to finish the job after she'd knocked the meddlesome bitch out.

"And you're insane. Now put it on the ground."

Her body stiffened. Not from fear so much as from resolve. She'd been in these situations before.

"And if I don't?"

"I'll send you back to the Devil."

Cadence smirked. "Suppose you put yours down first."

Shade leaned closer. "Why should I?"

"Because, if you don't, I'll kill Vogel."

* * *

"I'm an intelligence agent!" Vogel repeated to the first officer for the third time.

"So, where's your identification?" asked the second officer.

"I've already explained that to you! I'm undercover! We have a situation here."

"We're aware of the situation," a security guard cut in.

"Then get someone on that bridge!" Vogel yelled, pointing to it. "The shooter is up there right now and you're doing nothing!"

"We're asking you what you're doing here with a gun," said the first officer. "Are you part of the attempt on the Nouvik's life?"

Vogel looked at them in exasperation. "Will you listen to me? I'm an agent! The person you want is up there!" She whirled around, her instincts screaming, — and saw it a split second before it happened. The sharp glint of the rifle's muzzle. Then, the flash.

* * *

Malachai and Kaplan hurried the Nouvik roughly through the parking garage. The plan could still be salvaged, but there was no time to spare. They stopped suddenly at a nondescript black car and a door was quickly opened.

The Nouvik turned to Malachai. "You realize you will never get away with this."

"I believe we will."

Kaplan grabbed the Nouvik by the shoulder and began shoving him into the car.

"I wouldn't bet on that," said a voice from across the garage.

Malachai turned his head. The outline of two figures was visible.

* * *

Mason walked across the parking garage toward the group with Richard Davis following a step behind.

"Now, I don't believe this is particularly sporting," he said, reaching the car. "Do you, Mr. Davis?"

"Not a bit."

Malachai looked as if he were seeing things. "What on Earth are you doing here?"

"I could ask you the same thing. You know, abduction of international figures is really rather frowned upon these days."

"Not to mention attempted assassination," added Davis.

"Quite right."

Malachai bristled. "I don't have time for this. Vanish. Or we'll shoot you where you stand."

"That would be ill-advised," Mason said, glancing to one side. "Wouldn't you agree sir?!"

Archer stepped from the shadows and nodded. "I'm afraid the agency would consider it bad form. Particularly, under these circumstances." Other agents joined him on either side. Mason counted six in all. He turned back to Malachai, whose mouth was open in astonishment.

"The authorities," the Nouvik said, in relief. "I told you."

Malachai turned slowly to Mason, with a look of bewilderment. The pistol dropped absently from his hand. "It would seem as though—I have been outmatched."

Davis picked up the gun and Mason nodded to Malachai with a raised eyebrow. "Gin, as it were."

Archer approached and put a hand on Mason's shoulder. "You know, headquarters is going to raise hell about this. First Vogel and now you. Those Mayday codes are restricted to specific missions."

"So, they are."

"And active agents, I might add. You're making my job more complicated than it already is, Mason."

"Well, let's say I was feeling nostalgic."

Archer put a hand out as the other agents approached and Mason shook it. "What I want to know," said Archer, "is how you even remembered the thing?"

Mason gave a slight smile. "I kept it in my shoe. Had a feeling it might come in handy someday."

* * *

Kaplan stiffened as the intelligence officers approached. The pistol was still in his right hand and his left gripped the arm of the Nouvik.

This was not over.

"No!" he said, as one of the men came near. "Stay back!"

He spun the Nouvik around pointing the gun at his head. Malachai stared at him in shock. "Kaplan, what are you doing?"

"Saving the Revolution!" he said.

"You're mad," said the Nouvik. "All of you."

"Quiet!"

"Kaplan, it's over," said Malachai. "We've lost. There will be another time, but this won't help us. Put the gun down."

"No, it's not over!" Kaplan's grip on the Nouvik tightened. Panic clawed at him as reality sank in. He was surrounded. Malachai had betrayed him, and the revolution he fought for was slipping away. Desperate, Kaplan backed up, dragging the Nouvik with him, as a human shield. "Stay away!" he shouted. "All of you, stay away!"

* * *

Richard Davis stood at the side of the group watching everything. Mason and the others had forgotten his presence, but his reporter instincts told him the man holding the Nouvik hostage had only one option.

To run past him.

Davis looked at the pistol in his hand and swallowed. He had never fired a weapon at a human being before. But these people were dangerous, and they'd hurt Vogel.

Something had to be done.

* * *

Kaplan continued backing up, keeping the Nouvik in front of him. He was scared now. There was no one to give him orders and nowhere to go. He had one chance. They had passed a stairwell on their way to the car. If he could get to the stairwell, perhaps he could get away and contact the others.

"Kaplan, please," Malachai said. "Be reasonable."

Kaplan shook his head. He was trying to trick him. "No!"

"Son don't do this," whispered the Nouvik.

"All of you, shut up!!" Kaplan screamed. Shoving the Nouvik forward, he turned and started for the stairwell.

* * *

Davis held the gun at arm's length, steadying it with his other hand, just as Vogel had shown him.

It was chaos, as everyone rushed toward the Nouvik.

Kaplan darted past him at full speed and before Davis realized it, his forefinger had pulled the trigger.

Looking down he saw smoke drifting from the barrel of the gun.

* * *

Kaplan felt the bullet enter his body immediately. A sharp, searing pain. His body jerked, and he stumbled forward, vision blurring, finally collapsing onto the hard concrete. As darkness crept in, he realized Malachai had been right. The Revolution was over.

* * *

Officer Robbins charged down the hall and reached the entrance to the bridge. A security guard stood in front of the automatic doors.

"Can I help you?" the guard asked.

"Move!" said Robbins.

"I'm sorry, I can't do that, sir."

"I said, get out of the way!"

"The bridge is closed, sir. The doors are malfunctioning and—"

"Listen, you moron! There's been an attempt on the Nouvik's life! Haven't you been paying attention?! The shots came from this direction! Now, move out of the way before I arrest you for interfering with an investigation!"

He shoved past the man and forced the doors open. What he saw next would be burned into his memory forever. The bridge, eerily silent and empty, revealed two figures—suddenly materializing from nowhere. One, a blonde woman, laying lifeless, clutching a rifle. The other, the brown-haired woman from earlier, sat slumped against the railing. Her face pale and distant. A pistol dropped from her hand, as she glanced up at him with a vague expression.

"Is she alive?" she asked.

"Who?" Robbins said.

"Vogel."

"What is this?!" the security guard had apparently followed Robbins out onto the bridge. "This area is supposed to be closed. When did . . . oh my gosh!"

The brown-haired woman suddenly slipped into unconsciousness. Robbins whipped around, barking at the guard, "Get some help! Now!" He rushed over, dropping to his knees beside the unconscious woman.

"She's been shot!" said the guard.

"I said, get some help!" Robbins screamed.

* * *

The police dispatcher on duty that afternoon was a haggard man named Becker.

It was nearing the end of his shift and Becker wanted to go home. Odd reports had been coming in during the last twenty minutes from Vaughn University. He took another sip of coffee and readjusted his headset. The familiar static buzzed in his ear.

"Headquarters, this is Thompson, over."

Becker pushed a button on his control panel. "Thompson, this is headquarters, go ahead."

"We have a 10-67 on the premises. Request dispatch of . . . and . . . er."

Becker shook his head. He hated when this happened. Whatever Thompson was trying to report had been garbled. He needed a new radio, along with half of the department.

"Thompson, this is headquarters. Please repeat last transmission, over."

". . . 10-67 on-premises. Request an ambulance Subject . . . woman . . . shot and killed . . . intelligence agent Vogel . . . please advise. Over."

Chapter 20
One month later

Shade sat on the other side of the desk and looked absently around the office. It had been a long time since she'd sat in this chair. The knick-knacks and leather-bound volumes looked virtually the same, though, and she wondered if any of them had ever been opened.

Twelve continued reading a lengthy report through her librarian glasses. She made a note at one point, then closed the folder and looked up. Shade couldn't read her face.

"Quite an adventure, Agent Shade."

Shade nodded. "Rather."

"I don't need to state again our gratitude for your actions."

"Thank you."

"Your service to this country has been exemplary."

"It's my pleasure."

"I've sent a copy of your report to your superiors, along with my recommendation that you be reinstated immediately. They're anxious to have you back."

"That's very kind," said Shade.

"Not at all. It's the least I could do."

Shade crossed her legs. "What's the department going to do with the professor's invention?"

Twelve laid the folder aside. "Professor Blackmarr will be officially recognized for his contributions to scientific research and rewarded with a generous government grant. In exchange, he's agreed to redirect his focus to less... sensitive projects. As for his invention, all records and materials are now classified. It no longer exists. And I trust the professor will remember that."

Shade smirked. "I'd say he's earned a paid vacation."

"That's one of the perks."

The two women smiled. Twelve took off her glasses and looked across the desk with a softened expression. "Shade, I know you don't officially work for this department, but we feel as if you're one of our own. If there is ever anything I can do for you . . ."

"Vogel," said Shade. "She was—"

Twelve raised a hand. "I understand. It's been taken care of."

"Thank you."

"Is there anything else?" Twelve asked.

Shade paused and leaned forward. "Actually, there is one thing."

* * *

Mason sat at a table in the airport coffee shop and glanced at his watch for the second time. He added cream and sugar to his coffee and stirred. As he took a sip, Shade sat down across from him.

"I'm sorry I'm late," she said. "I haven't traveled for a while."

"I was afraid you might miss the flight."

Shade smiled. "It was close."

"Going back home, are you?"

"Yes. Twelve all but offered me a job, but home is home. They need me there."

He put down the coffee and looked serious for a moment. "Shade, I'm not very good at saying 'thank you,' but what you did back there . . ." She looked uncomfortable and he paused. "Well, it was 'noble.'"

A slow smile spread across her face. "Thank you," she said. "You weren't entirely ignoble yourself, Mason. In fact, you were downright, chivalrous, if I might use the term."

Mason raised an eyebrow. "You caught me on a bad day, I'm afraid."

"I doubt that. I think maybe you're hiding your light under a bushel."

He managed a dry smile. "Point taken."

They sat awkwardly for a moment, and she thumbed the edge of her purse. "Well, I should probably be going. I wouldn't want to miss the plane."

"No, of course not." She started out of the chair, and he stood with her. "Listen. Before you go—"

Shade looked at him. "Yes?"

Mason cleared his throat. "What I mean is, over there, back home, do you—have anyone? Anyone—significant."

A smile played across her face, and she turned to him. "No, Mason, I don't. Why?"

"Well," he stammered. "I just thought that maybe sometime, if schedules permitted, perhaps—"

"Perhaps we could have dinner?"

Mason nodded. "Perhaps."

For a brief moment, the smile faltered, replaced by something softer. "Perhaps." Then, with a look that seemed to say many things, she exited the coffee shop.

Mason watched as her silhouette disappeared into the crowd, straining for one final look.

"Very touching," a familiar voice cut through his thoughts. "Almost poetic, in a way."

He didn't flinch, but the shift in his expression was subtle. He turned to see a man in a tailored suit standing at his table.

"You always did have terrible timing, Kingston," Mason said coolly. "I was just catching up with an old friend."

"Indeed. Well, I'm here to discuss certain other 'friends.'"

He eyed the man carefully. "And here I thought I'd earned myself a vacation."

"What would be the fun in that?"

Mason didn't answer right away. Instead, he picked up his coffee, watching the light reflect off the dark liquid.

Kingston chuckled. "You know, I think you're losing your edge, old boy. Between that minx and your little detour with Vogel—"

"Vogel's not part of this equation," Mason looked up, the smile gone. "And I haven't lost anything."

The man in the suit raised an eyebrow. "Well, that's a start." He dropped a few bills on the table and moved past him. "We'll be in touch."

"I'll be waiting," he said, his eye following him. He took one last sip of his coffee. It was only then that he realized he'd forgotten to ask Shade for her name.

* * *

The Nouvik of Arden closed the thick volume in his lap and looked thoughtfully out the window of his study. Sunlight streamed in and from his vantage point he could see trees and a robin's-egg blue sky, with just a wisp of cloud. There was a knock at the door.

"Yes?"

It opened and Andrew entered, carrying a tray on which rested a teapot, cups, and a plate of pastries. "Your tea, sir."

"Of course. Just set it anywhere."

Andrew put the tray down on a small table and stood awkwardly beside it.

The Nouvik glanced at him. "Is there anything else?"

"Sir?"

"Well, you have the look of a man with something on his mind."

Andrew hesitated. "Actually, I've been thinking."

"About?"

"About what happened at the university."

"I see."

He fumbled with his hands and walked over to the Nouvik's chair. "Sir, they were going to kill you!"

"Yes, they were."

"In cold blood."

"So, it would seem."

"And yet you don't seem—affected by any of this."

"That's not true, Andrew," the Nouvik said, laying the book aside. "It was an absolutely terrifying experience. But also, an eye-opening one."

"What do you mean?"

"That government woman, the one who threw me to the ground?"

"Agent Vogel?"

"Exactly. She was willing to die to save my life. A complete stranger. That's eye-opening, Andrew."

"Yes, it is. When someone has the audacity to shoot at a figure such as yourself, it proves that the world has become a truly dangerous and violent place."

The Nouvik shook his head. "That's not what I meant. The world has always been dangerous, and there have always been those who chose violence. But the fact that that Vogel woman was willing to risk her life for mine is encouraging."

"Encouraging?" Andrew said, with a perplexed look.

"Encouraging because it shows that some are listening. Some are still concerned for the greater good and willing to take action to preserve it. I was looking for a sign, Andrew. And I think I may have gotten it."

Andrew gave him a confused expression. "So, you feel it was a sign? A positive thing?"

"Yes," the Nouvik said, his voice gaining a rare firmness." A sign that maybe I should do more than watch. Maybe I should start taking action myself. That other woman, the one from T.I. who disarmed the sniper?"

"Agent Shade?"

"Agent Shade, exactly. We'll start with her. I'd like to speak with her as soon as she returns."

"An official meeting," Andrew nodded. "I understand. I'll arrange it at once."

"Make that unofficial."

"Your grace?"

"As unofficial as possible."

"I'm afraid I don't understand."

284

"Let's just say that Miss Shade is going to be given the opportunity to talk about anything she likes. And I'm going to sit and listen for a change."

"With all due respect, sir, the Nouvik of Arden is renowned for his wisdom. Shouldn't she—"

"Andrew," the Nouvik said, standing up. "Silence is the beginning of wisdom. Now, let's have tea."

* * *

Hanover sat in the dirty visitor cubicle of the Maximum-security prison, with its grimy, two-way phone and waited. He did not like being in places like this, but it was necessary.

He looked up as the guard led Malachai to a seat on the other side of the thick plexiglass. Malachai picked up his receiver and Hanover did the same.

"Hanover?" said Malachai.

"Malachai?"

"It's good to see you again."

"You as well. How have you been?"

"Not bad, all things considered. This place has a certain amount of rustic charm if you can learn to tolerate the—well, it would be a mistake to call it food."

Hanover lowered his voice. "We need to talk, Malachai. There have been some developments at the higher level."

Malachai leaned in. "How so?"

"I'd rather not go into it here. Let's just say recent events have raised concern."

"What kinds of concern?"

"Grave concern."

Malachai gave him a surprised look. "You mean they want to leave me here?"

"It's been discussed."

"By whom?"

"I'm not going to say. But I think you need to be aware of the severity of the situation. It's entirely possible that you're going to be handed your hat."

The guard walked by, and Malachai whispered into the mouthpiece. "Hanover, you've got to get me out of here! The only way I can convince them of anything is in person!"

"I'm trying, Malachai, but it's not easy. That fiasco with Vogel was—"

"Vogel is dead, Hanover. Tell them that."

Hanover stared at him. "You're positive of this?"

"Absolutely."

"What about Shade?"

"Shade is irrelevant. Besides, what I have in mind will give us plenty of opportunities to deal with her if we wish."

Hanover nodded slowly. "I can tell them that. Just be patient, Malachai. These things can take time."

"Patience is a virtue, Hanover."

* * *

Richard Davis pulled into the parking lot of The Lancaster Chronicle and turned off the engine. It was a Saturday morning, and his was the only car. He sat in the front seat for several minutes looking at nothing. Finally, he climbed out and closed the door. The sky was overcast, and the sea salt smell of the ocean hung in the air. Davis put a hand to his temple and massaged it. His head hurt. It had been a late night. There had been a lot of late nights, ever since . . .

He began walking toward the office. His editor had relaxed considerably since the call from Washington. His assignments now included feature stories and his desk had been moved to a private office. There had even been a salary increase.

Cathy had even forgiven him. For the most part.

But even that didn't matter anymore. He simply wasn't interested.

Not now.

A mild sprinkle had started, and Davis felt in his pocket for keys. He found them and unlocked the storefront office. Stepping inside, he switched on the light and looked for coffee. An empty pot sat on the burner. He would get to that later. Right now, he just wanted to sit and think. Let his mind cool and put it all down on paper. From start to finish. No interruptions.

He took the spiral notebook from the paper bag and felt in his coat for a pen. Walking to his office, he opened the door and flipped another light switch. As the light came on, Davis froze in his tracks.

She was sitting in the chair across from his desk.

"Hello, Richard Davis."

The notebook fell to the floor.

"Vogel . . ."

The End

Paul G. Wright is a native of Atlanta, GA. He has worked as a newspaper journalist, freelance writer, and screenwriter. He studied acting at the Warehouse Actors Theater and earned his degree in filmmaking from Columbia College Hollywood, in Tarzana, CA. He currently resides in the Atlanta area with his wife and their cat Dusty.

bwlpublishing.ca

Made in the USA
Columbia, SC
23 December 2024